**His children had been kidnapped, and harmed. Some-
one would have to pay…**

"Mr. Sattill a guy just dropped off a package for you and the missus."

"I'll be right down, thanks."

The small box is wrapped in plain brown paper. The word, "Sattill" is scrawled on one side. The reverse side is taped. The box weighs next to nothing yet something moves back and forth as Tony gently shakes the package. The elevator to his foyer opens, and Tony is met by his team, sans Melissa.

"Let's open this in the kitchen on the big table. I'm sure this is not a bomb, but other than that, I have no idea what's inside. I want the paper checked for prints. The door men in the building wear white gloves, so any prints will be the delivery man."

Tony judiciously cuts the tape and unfolds the paper surrounding the box. He hands the paper to Chris, who is calling his precinct for a messenger to pick up the paper and run it for prints. The box is approximately four inches by four inches. Plain white. Purchasable in any drug store or card shop. No clues to follow. Tony delicately removes the top and sees the message. His heart sinks.

Wrapped in tissue or toilet paper is the bloody finger of a child. He guesses it's the pinky.

"What's going on in here? Who's making coffee?"

"Sweetie, I'm not sure you want to be here now. We can discuss this later."

"What's in the box? I want to see."

Her scream is nearly ear shattering. She instantly turns to walk away, but spins around to more closely inspect the mutilated appendage.

Tony Sattill has retired a captain from the NYPD Manhattan Crime Analysis Team (CAT). He lives well with his wife, Melissa, and their three children in the penthouse of his wife's former husband. He lectures on the value of CAT to out-of-town police departments. With the killing of a former CAT member, Tony jumps back into his familiar aggressive police mode. Over the course of the next weeks, there are several seemingly unrelated murders. Working with the remaining members of his CAT, Tony connects the dots. The Archangels Motorcycle Club and four paroled Ethiopians are visible elements of a criminal cabal. Tony requests of the NYPD that he be the "go to guy" in determining the goal of this complex and violent group. In his ego-driven quest, he receives help from Paul Tybor, who works from the shadows. Tony's two sons and daughter are growing up, as evidence by their school activities. The closer Tony gets to the truth about the cabal, the more violence rains. Starting with a massive fire fight in the Colorado desert, this violence culminates in the kidnapping of his children. He attempts to rescue them, but with chilling results…

KUDOS for *Vengeance*

In *Vengeance* by John Andes, Tony Sattill of the NYPD is back. He has retired as a captain, but when bodies start piling up associated with an old case, Tony wants back in. He is married now and has three children, and his involvement puts his family in danger. Can he solve this new case before more innocent lives are taken? Like the first book in the series, this one is intense, fast paced, and chilling. You won't be able to put it down. *~ Taylor Jones, The Review Team of Taylor Jones & Regan Murphy*

Vengeance by John Andes is the story of Tony Sattill, a captain in the NYPD, whom we first met in *Hidden Agenda*. Tony has retired from the force, has married, and has a family. He has three children, a beautiful wife, and life couldn't be better. Then members of a team he worked with on a case fifteen years ago start dying. As the team members continue to be murdered, Tony demands to be let in on the case, putting his own life and those of his family at risk. Has he gotten more than he bargained for this time? Well written, fast paced, and full of surprises, *Vengeance* will thrill even the most hardened police procedural mystery fans. A really great read. *~ Regan Murphy, The Review Team of Taylor Jones & Regan Murphy*

VENGEANCE

John Andes

A Black Opal Books Publication

GENRE: MYSTERY-DETECTIVE/POLICE PROCEDURAL

This is a work of fiction. Names, places, characters and incidents are either the product of the author's imagination or are used fictitiously, and any resemblance to any actual persons, living or dead, businesses, organizations, events or locales is entirely coincidental. All trademarks, service marks, registered trademarks, and registered service marks are the property of their respective owners and are used herein for identification purposes only. The publisher does not have any control over or assume any responsibility for author or third-party websites or their contents.

نتقــــام الا

Chapter 1

Ding. Ding.

The strange alarm clock ring stirs Tony. Then the voice bridges the gap between sleep and awakened reality.

"Ladies and gentlemen, the captain has turned on the fasten seat belt sign. Please make sure your seat belt s fastened and your tables and seat backs are in their upright positions as we approach our final destination, LaGuardia Airport in New York City.

How many times has Tony heard that request? He wonders if the young woman on the speaker system is the daughter or niece of the first woman he heard give the same instructions. Gawd, he has been flying too many years. To unfold his body, he stretches his legs and back, tilts his head to both sides, and bends forward at the waist while counting to ten. Rubbing the sleep from his eyes and blowing his nose completes the ritual. He needs a hot towel for his face. No such luck.

"The cabin crew will be passing through the aisle to collect any cups, glasses, and paper trash you may have. Thank you for your cooperation.

Somehow sleeping in a seated position on an airplane is not relaxing. He is anxious to get home to his own bed and his own wife. Reports are due tomorrow. More importantly, he must spend time with Antonio, Bartheleme, and Cassandra when their school day is completed. Should dad take them to the Cone and Scoop and ruin their dinner, thus garnering the mock wrath of their mother. The family will eat at seven-thirty not six, and Tony will perform some form of adult atonement. Jesus, he is already planning tomorrow, without consulting Melissa. That approach is doomed from the start. He must wait to hear her plans for the day.

"Ladies and gentlemen, this is Captain Wessells. We're making our final approach to LaGuardia Airport. Please be sure your seat belts are securely fastened. We'll be on the ground in eight minutes. For all of us on the flight deck and in the cabin, we know you have air travel choices, and we're pleased you chose American Airlines for this trip. In the future, if your plans call for air travel, think American first. Thank you and have a pleasant rest of your stay in the New York area or wherever your final destination is. Cabin crew, cross check"

Make sure his bag is still beneath the seat in front of him. Extract it. Open the outer zippered pocket and insert lecture notes.

"Ladies and gentlemen, we'll be on the ground momentarily. Please look around your seat to be sure you have all your belongings. Upon landing, please remain seated until the captain has turned off the seat belt sign and the airplane is safely docked at the gate. Do not stand to retrieve your bag from the overhead compartment. There'll be plenty of time to retrieve your bag once we're docked. For all of the cabin crew, it has been a pleasure serving you. In the future, if your plans call for air travel, think American first. The local time is eleven fifty-five p.m., Eastern Standard Time. Have a pleasant evening."

The lights from the ground rush up to meet the plane as it approaches a tall building above the tarmac. Two small bounces and he is home. Then the long and labored taxi ride to the gate. It seems his gate is in Hartford. Two bells indicate he had safely arrived, but still the seat belt sign is lit. Some people stand, open the overhead compartments, and retrieve their bags. Then the seat belt light is extinguished. The mad house of hurry up and wait is in full swing. Hell, he gets out when he gets out. No earthly reason to stand and wait. First class exits immediately, then business class—that's him—and finally those in steerage. The entire process takes twelve minutes. But with anxiety levels high, some feel as if it takes an hour.

Up the ramp to the staging area. Turn right and walk deliberately down the long hall. The plane arrived at Gate A-1. Ground transportation is down the stairs from Gate A-32. Pass by the ubiquitous shops that sell newspapers, candy, and magazines, Aunt Fannies Pretzels, and "I Love New York" T-shirts and trinkets, as well all manner of fast food eateries. They are all closed for the night. The shoe shine booth is locked. The many doors marked "Do Not Enter. Alarm Will Sound. Employees Only." Each door has a button key pad at its side that will open the door and deactivate the alarm.

The maintenance personnel are sweeping, vacuuming, and dusting to make ready for tomorrow. Music plays softly and the aroma of people and fast food fills his nostrils. The only people in the hall are walking out. But there are people at the gates' staging areas. They are resting on the floor or reading. They are waiting for the first flight out in the morning. Did they miss the last flight? Their countenances are vaguely reminiscent of the Jews in concentration camps. A blank expression of resignation. Waiting and enduring are components of their fate. Gawd, he's taken this way too far.

The escalator ride to ground transportation opens the vista of a milling but quiet mob. There is Adolfo. He recognizes Tony, smiles, and waves politely. Tony nod. He takes the bag. Not so heavy that the passenger could not carry it easily, but Adolfo is mindful of small niceties. He opens the rear door to the Mercedes stretch. The large leather seats and the solid door closing are comforting. It smells familiar.

"How was your trip, Mr. Sattill?"

"Pleasant because it was short and my audience was interested in what I had to say. Three days is long enough. I miss my family. I miss New York. It is good to see other cities, so that I can compare them to mine. Los Angeles has great weather, worse traffic than New York, and air that you could cut with a very dull knife. It is good to be home. Tell me—any crises? "

"None that I know of, sir."

Adolfo was hired soon after Tony's marriage to Melissa. Tony wanted her and Antonio to be safe and comfortable as they moved about Manhattan. Safety was a critical factor for the family of an NYPD captain. Melissa luxuriated in the pampering. And as Bartheleme and Cassandra appeared, grew, and wanted all sorts of transportation, Adolfo and the stretch were a necessary household expense. Adolfo was hired as a favor to the Colucci family in Brooklyn. He was just out of prison. The eight-year aggravated assault and battery hitch was over. According to the state, he had been rehabilitated and was permitted to re-enter society—with certain restrictions. The boss, Franco Colucci, felt Adolfo needed a break and reached out to Tony, a fellow Brooklynite. Franco is known as "The Face" because of his very good looks. The capos and the police call him The Face, while everyone else calls him Mr. Colucci. Adolfo was well-taken care of and very loyal. His ties to the family had been severed. Hopefully.

It is a nice to enjoy the perks of the Razdarovich money without the hassle of the Razdarovich family. The retired captain never lost sight of the irony that he helped put an end to the family's influence on the city. To the victor belong the spoils. The ride is an effortless thirty-five minutes. The doorman greets Tony and takes his bag to the elevator. The key to his private floor is inserted. With one turn of the key, the door closes and the chariot begins to carry the tired traveler home.

As the elevator doors open, she, in all her beauty stands before him. She is wearing her silk pajamas. She knows how much he likes her in her silk pajamas. Melissa wraps her arms around his chest and kisses him deeply. There is something good in store for both of them.

"How are the children?"

"The little darlings have been a pain in the ass. I'm not sure I, or they, will live through the prepubescent and puberty years. The hormonal rushes are like a curse from some very nasty god somewhere. Antonio's the worst. Girls and guy stuff occupy his every waking minute. Were you like that?"

"No I was a perfectly behaved altar boy. May we get adult beverages from the kitchen and continue this conversation in the bedroom? Then you can tell me all that has happened during my three-day absence. Oh, and by-the-by, Retired Captain Anthony Sattill's West Coast tour went well."

Shower after unpacking, which really means tossing some clothes in the laundry hamper and the socially acceptable clothes in the dry cleaner bag. Running shorts and Brown University T-shirt are regular sleeping clothes. The couple sits on the big bed and sips the remainder of the Balvenie.

"Now, tell me, how bad were the children?"

"I guess they were typical fifteen, fourteen, and twelve-year-olds. It's just that they miss you, and they take out their frustration on me. And, as an only child, I had not been prepared for behavior like that. You'll see it at breakfast. Squabbling, picking, bitching, whining, and some physical interaction. Meals are like feeding time on the Savannah. Hopefully, now that papa lion is home, the pride will behave or, or least, listen to me knowing I have your visible support. That's enough about my days. How was the lecture?"

"Many large city police departments have a CAT squad or something similar. Therefore the lecture attendees are interested in any nuances they can glean from my experiences. The Q and A part of the lectures are the most telling. I learn of cases on which they're working. Particular issues they face. Conundrums they can't solve. Sometimes I can help. Sometimes not. It seems the LAPD is struggling with a serial killer, who targets Yuppies after they leave their gyms or spas. No specific time of day. Just after they leave their health clubs. And not the same health clubs. Never their homes. The health club business is declining so rapidly, here is fear that it will die off completely if the police do not solve the murders. I can't go into more detail. This is where confidentiality becomes a force.

San Diego is experiencing a rash of brutal, near-death muggings of men and women in the financial sectors. Bankers. Stock brokers. Insurance executives. Never death, just beatings. The executives have hired bodyguards and drivers. This makes them obvious in the populace. San Francisco has murders that look like they were by one of the Chinese gangs. This, I think, is a case of deflected responsibility. But who is doing the deflection? Enough. Enough. Enough."

The Balvenie is working its magic, muscles are relaxing, eyelids are getting heavier, and lust is growing in two loins. Lights are turned off and bodies are turned on. Kisses that start sweet and tender take on urgency. Hands slide over two bodies. Sleeping clothes are gently, but firmly removed, and bodies become engaged. Horizontal thrashing morphs into rhythmic wave like motions. Bliss is reached and breathing becomes deep and normal.

"I love you, Melissa."

"Back attatchya, Anthony."

⁊⁊⁊

Well-deserved slumber is crashed by two caterwauling off-spring. Banging on the sanctuary door as they open it, they give barely enough time for the adults to pull on tops. Bartheleme and Cassandra leap onto the big bed and scream, "Daddy's home."

Tony gets hugs and kisses from Cassandra and guy-to-guy shoulder punches from Bartheleme. Melissa is ignored. She does not feel slighted. She has time and space to pull on her thong and pajama bottoms.

"Okay. Okay. Okay. I missed you guys, too. Where is Antonio?"

"That lazy bum is still asleep in the upper bunk. He calls it his aerie. You know an eagle's nest that no other bird can attack."

"Well, Bartheleme, shall we attack the eagle's nest and get big bird out? Cassie, you have first turn in the bathroom, while we roust the raptor."

Four bodies leave the bed—Daddy and Bartheleme to the boys' room, Cassie, to the children's bathroom, and Melissa to the kitchen. Children need food and adults need coffee. The two males charge through the door of the boys' room. Tony jumps up to see the denizen of the top bunk, while Bartheleme climbs the ladder at the foot of the bunk.

"Arise Antonio and join us for breakfast or suffer the consequences."

"Leave me alone, Dad. I'm tired. I don't feel well. I may be coming down with something."

"Back in my days on the force it was called the Blue Flu. It was a bogus sickness related reason to avoid work. The epidemic most often occurred during contract negotiations. If the negotiations were not going the PBA's way, the Blue Flu was a tactic to show New Yorkers how valuable their police force was and dangerous the city would be if the police force was treated badly. The ploy never worked then and it won't work now. Get your butt out of the sack or I will climb up there and cover you with kisses until you flee your nest screaming."

"Rats! You win. Give me two minutes, and I'll be in the kitchen."

Morning tumescence dissipates rapidly in young teens.

The breakfast table is set for the darlings. Cassandra, café mocha skinned, is beginning to look exactly like her mother. She will be drop dead gorgeous soon. That will be an issue when puberty hits. Bartheleme, café con leche in color, is a blend of his mother and father. His mother's slender build and his father's nose and chin. His mind and body are still fighting over his outcome. Antonio, except for his color, is my child. His chest jond legs are beginning to develop. He is already five feet ten inches, his face is Mediterranean, and his hair is soft and wavy.

Melissa has reminded Ton numerous times that he has to have "the talk" with him before it is too late. She has indicated that his phone seems to be permanently attached to his hands. If he is not texting, he is conducting a spy-like conversation. Recently she accidentally came upon him gazing wantonly at a photo attachment to an e-mail from a girl in the grade above him. Dad can read the signs. Soon, "the talk". Tony would rather have his teeth drilled by an angry Nazi dentist, but he owes it to Melissa, Antonio, and his marriage.

The three enter together. All are talking at once and each attempts to talk above the others. The cacophony is nearly ear shattering.

"Whoa, strangers. In this saloon we speak with civility and we don't interrupt. If these rules are not followed, the saloon keeper and his wife will toss you out into the muddy cattle path. Understand?"

Begrudgingly, they acknowledge the demand.

"Who wants cereal? Who wants a muffin?"

Melissa has devised a simple breakfast plan—a protein drink, an orange or apple, a glass of two-percent milk and either cereal or a muffin. These latter two are the same ingredients, just different delivery systems. The kitchen is not her comfort zone.

"Anthony. Bartheleme. Get ready for school. You may take your muffin into your room. Adolfo will be here in ten minutes."

Actually, Adolfo will be here to drive them the ten blocks to Heavenly Rest Academy in twenty minutes. But, like dogs and cats, young children have no real sense of time. The front door opens. It is Carmelita, here to ensure that the house is clean and orderly, and that the larder is filled with the needs of her adopted family.

"Buenos, Carmelita."

"Good morning to you, Mr. Sattill."

Our greeting is interrupted by the thundering herd as they head to the elevator and lobby.

"See you guys after school."

"Tony, can we have a civil cup of coffee in the sun-room?"

"Indeed."

Tony brings the small wooden box that contains the unopened family correspondence. He is always amazed at how trash mail arrives in my absence. Many of the envelopes contain bills. Retiring with a captain's pension and a personal investment accounts, plus lecture fees have afforded a nice individual income. Nothing like Melissa's. She got tons from the Latchazar Razdarovich estate. When Melissa and Tony were married, they agreed to share, on a pro rata basis, expenses insofar as their incomes would allow. The division of income seems equitable, because it makes him feel less like he is being kept, and she absolutely loves spending Lucky's money.

"What's on your agenda for the day?"

"The spa at ten, then to the shelter to serve lunch and a board meeting. I'll be there until four. And, you?"

"I want to work on my notes, and try to incorporate some of the questions posed during my recent trip. Plus, I need to answer requests from several cities for speaking engagement. I'll try to schedule them in clumps to cut down on the day trips. I want to get in a run. I'm rusty after three days on the lecture circuit. Then a nap. Remember, I'm retired. There's no urgency to my work."

"What would you like for dinner? I need to tell Carmelita, so she can buy the food and cook it before she leaves."

"Pulled pork, Spanish rice, and black beans."

"You're so predictable."

"But I love it, and Carmelita's is fantastic. Beside that way you don't have to cook, and I'll clean up. I'm just making life easy for my adorable wife."

"Did I also mention that you're so full of it that your eyes are brown?"

"I love you, too, sweetie."

"I hate to gulp and bolt, but Sven, my new trainer, gets pissed if I'm late."

"Should I be jealous of Sven?"

"Only if you find a seventy-year-old threatening."

"Before you go, do we have time to—"

"*No*! Save that thought for tonight."

The early morning sun is beginning to warm my space under the sky that is protected from the elements. Tony settles into opening the bills. The ringing of his phone interrupts the reverie.

"Captain, this is Brendan."

"Lieutenant McLaughlin, how are you?"

"Have you read the paper or watched TV this morning?"

"No."

"The transit cops and Homeland Security discovered the body of a woman, who had been killed at LaGuardia. She was found in one of the stair wells. Her throat was slit and she had been molested."

"Yes. What has that to do with you and me?"

"It was—she was Jamie, Jamie Lanno. She was one of us. Now she's dead. Slaughtered. What can we do?"

Chapter 2

A huge knot suddenly appeared in Tony's stomach. A knot like the ones suffered when he first came upon a mutilated body or when someone he knew became a statistic. This was different. This was Jamie—one of the team. Smart, tough, and thorough. Tony had heard that, after he left the department, she was promoted to lieutenant and had transferred to sex crimes—something she truly wanted. She wanted to help victims, not just speak for the dead.

"Brendan, are you sure?"

"Positive. The official report has not been issued yet. The brass is notifying her parents and Cherie. I spoke to Jamie a few weeks ago. She was so happy and excited. She and Cherie were given the green light to adopt a child. Jamie wanted to see her parents face-to-face and tell them the good news. Her folks were about to be grandparents."

"Does Chris know?"

"Not positive, but most likely. If the Bronx knows, Brooklyn knows."

"What details can you give me?"

"Not much beyond the official announcement."

"I'd like to know what details are being left out of the announcement. Who's handling the case?"

"The investigation is being handled by a team of detectives from Queens with the support of the borough CAT lieutenant, Thomason," Brendon says. "You remember him. He is the one who pissed and moaned loudly that you got all the glory cases and the promotion to captain, while he got bupkus and remained in Queens. He really resented your success."

"So, the official announcement will be made by ten, then radio silence. I'd like to know what is left out of the news reports. There is always something left out. Do some digging—quietly and learn what the department doesn't want the public to know. And be sure to call Chris. We'll reconvene via conference call at two this afternoon."

"Where are you going with this, Captain?"

"Not sure, yet. But I want to know everything about the murder of our Jamie."

Christ, she was such good person.

The phone calls again.

"Captain, have you heard about Jamie?"

"Yes, Brendan just called. What do you know?"

"I read the official report that came to us all via e-mail. I also heard she was mutilated in some sexual manner. Her work in sex crimes could have something to do with the murder."

"Mutilated? How?"

"The scuttlebutt is that her clitoris was hacked off. Not surgical, but butchery. My source at the ME's office neither confirmed nor denied the mutilation. But she did say that damage was done to the body, post mortem. That's all I know."

"I asked Brendan to dig into the situation. I ask you

to do the same. The three of us should compare notes at two today. Okay?"

"One more factor, Captain, is that the case is being handled by CAT lieutenant, Thomason. He was not a big fan of you or us. And you know he is very territorial. My guess is that he will want exclusivity on the investigation. Won't want to share a damned thing with outsiders, particularly retired outsiders, who were promoted over him."

"I'm keenly aware of the potential for friction and exclusion. I need to find a way in that he can't fight. Like working in a subordinate manner. Talk to you at two."

How to get in the back door without creating a departmental brouhaha is a puzzle. Kelly has long since retired, but only after his last big case. Tony really doesn't have any friends among the old timers at One PP. He thought they feared him. The tried and true always fear the rogues who get shit done and not always by the book. Maybe a captain who has been recently transferred to desk duty. Someone in his class at the Academy, who has had nothing to do with CAT or murder investigations. Valentino? LaRue? Paul? Who? Time to dial and smile.

"Captain LaRue's office."

"This is Captain Sattill. Is she there?"

"Just a second and I'll see."

"Anthony Sattill Captain NYPD Retired, how are you? How has life been treating you in your new celebrity status?"

"Jodi, it's good to talk to you. Life is good. The lecture circuit sucks. Flights to nowhere. Strange beds. Rich food. I fear all of this will have a bad impact on my health. What are you up to?"

"Catchin' robbers. Workin' toward retirement. Just doin' time on planet earth."

"Jodi I need your advice on a delicate matter."

"Yes, I guess you do."

"By now you're aware, that the victim at LaGuardia was one of ours. More than that, Jamie Lanno was a team mate of mine before I retired and she was promoted to sex crimes. What I need is a way in. A way that is acceptable to the force and most particularly Thomason. Can you help? I need suggestions."

"Thomason has a rabbi at One PP—Commander Terry Vincent. He might be able to suggest that Thomason let you in, because it's in Thomason's best interest to do so. You'll need a very big carrot. No stick allowed. You'll need a carrot for Vincent. As to the force, you'll have to go the Oversight Board, the grand poohbahs, who make, bend and break the rules. They'll need a really good reason to let you in. The really good reason would be a request from Thomason and Vincent. So, my friend, you'll have to convince the Bully of Queens simply to get a hearing. That'll be impossible without a big payoff for him guaranteed by and for Vincent. You have a lot of back scratching or ass kissing in your immediate future"

"Ah, the court of Medici, the efforts of Machiavelli, and the plight of Sattill. Italians all. One last question. How do I get to Vincent?

"Almost legal bribery might be a way. I understand Vincent has a small cottage in the Berkshires. You know, the classic "fuck you, I'm leaving" place. He paid top dollar for it near the height of the real estate boom. Sunk a ton of his savings into it. Upgrading it to a real house. All new stuff. The real estate market tanked. His pension was adjusted by the city. He's upside down on the mortgage and does not have the resources to cover his nut. I understand he keeps borrowing from his pension just to stay slightly behind. I suspect he would be eternally grateful to someone who became interested in his cottage and was willing to purchase the place for cash."

"How the hell did you learn all of this?"

"Do you really want to know?"

"One more question. Where in the Berkshires?"

"Pittsfield, Mass."

"Thanks, Jodi. I owe you big time."

"You can pay me after I retire by getting me some speaking gigs. Get me on the lecture circuit. I'll take payment in two years. Good luck. Say hello to Melissa for me."

A few hundred thousand dollars spent on a back door hunch that will take a minimum of three months to close. Not a good idea to start. But this might be a fallback position if the internal investigation goes nowhere and Tony can get Melissa to bankroll the venture. Hold this for three-four weeks. In the interim Brendan, Chris, and Tony will have to work their internal sources.

⌘

Ring, ring, ring.

"Hello."

"Captain, this is Brendan. Were you asleep?"

"Yeah, jet lag. Just a little nap. What did you learn?"

"Let conference in Chris. Chris, are you there?"

"Brendan? Captain?"

"Here's what I learned. Thomason is playing it close to the vest. But the riding detective has indicated that Jamie was really chopped up. Throat slit, cheeks cut, and a big gash on her chest. Obviously, a crime of passion, given that fact that she was working sex crimes. Her case log will be the first place they look. That may take weeks or months, given the nature of the cases she was working and the ACLU."

"Chris. Captain. My source in the ME's office let me know that the perp was more vicious that you just described. He took her clitoris as a trophy. How sick is that?

All precincts have been alerted to the slaughter, but not this last part. Captain, what did you find out about us getting involved?"

"There is a way, but it is very complicated and will take at least two to three months."

"What do we do now, Captain?"

"You two continue to gather information, I'll work on other angles, and we'll just stay in the background."

Back to his notes and audience questions. The sun is warm, the chair is comfortable, and eyelids are heavy. The minutia is like a drug. It cannot be fought.

⁊◦⁊

Ring, ring, ring.

A brief respite interrupted by my umbilical cord to the world. No rest for the weary. Or is that "the wicked"?

"Tony, good afternoon. This is Jerome Aylir."

"Good day to you, sir."

Tony hears from his father-in-law only when it is about seeing the grandchildren.

"How were your speaking engagements?"

"They went well, but I'm glad to be home with Melissa and the three-headed hydra. How can I help you, Jerry?"

"It's the other way. I want to help you. I understand that Jamie Lanno, who used to work with your CAT team, was found murdered at LaGuardia. I can only image how much this angers and disturbs you. You want to help with the investigation, but you're a civilian now and by definition kept out of the loop. I think I can help you with this. I still have some juice at One PP. If you're interested, I could ask around and see if there is a willingness on the part of the inhabitants of the hallowed halls to allow you to observe the investigation as a sort of 'thank you' for services rendered."

Tony's heart begins to race. "Sir, I would be eternally grateful if you could apply some friendly persuasion to the big brass. Allow me to tell you what I know. Lieutenant Thomason of Queens caught the case. He holds a grudge against me for the two high profile cases that lead to my promotion to captain. Plus, he is more territorial than a male Cardinal. He has a rabbi at One PP, who really pulls his strings. Commander Terry Vincent. He doesn't care for me because of the help given me by Kelly a few years back. I think Kelly trumped Vincent's ace a few times. These two men are high hurdles against me getting in on the investigation. But I know a way that is slightly illegal."

"Stop! Nothing illegal, unethical, or immoral. I think this can be resolved politically. I can ask around in a very pointed manner. A favor for you. A favor for me. And favors for Thomason and Vincent. Let us not forget my years of helping to run the city. I still have many favors to call in."

"Thank you, Jerry."

"I should have an answer for you when your family is here for dinner on Friday. It's been three weeks since we've seen the children. Jessica reminds me of this fact daily. So take some pressure off a fellow husband. Dinner on Friday?"

"Yes sir. Please tell Jessica thank you for the invitation. We'll be there at six. I'll let Melissa know of the plans."

Tony calls Chris and Brendan, reminds them to continue to dig without being obvious, and tells them of their new back door.

♋

"Bong. Bong. Bong. Newark. Newark. Change here for the Coast Line and the Jersey Central. This the last stop for the PATH trains. All exit. Change here for the Coast Line and the Jersey Central. Bong. Bong. Bong. Newark. Newark. Change here for the Coast Line and the Jersey Central. This the last stop for the PATH trains. All exit. Change here for the Coast Line and the Jersey Central. Next Coast Line train leaves from track five in twenty minutes. The next Jersey Central train leaves from track two in twenty minutes. Next Coast Line train leaves from track five in twenty minutes. The next Jersey Central train leaves from track two in twenty minutes. Track five for the next Coast Line train and track two for the next Jersey Central train. Track five for the next Coast Line train and track two for the next Jersey Central train. Look around your seat for your belongings. Please take all your belongings with you. Look around your seat for your belongings. Please take all your belongings with you. This is the final stop for the PATH train. All exit. Have a pleasant evening. This is the final stop for the PATH train. All exit. Have a pleasant evening."

The recorded message is the cue for passengers to gather up their newspapers, attaché cases, and beverage containers. They stand at the ready. Eyes glance at those who they have seen many times before. The same people take the same train and sit in the same car five evenings each week. Some are young men and women just starting their careers. Some are older men on the downside of their careers. They hope to extract a few more salaried years from the jobs before they are replaced by the young people who ride their train.

Then there are the middle-aged, middle management people who moved here looking for a way to conserve their incomes in a dangerously fluctuating economy. Groups will walk rapidly to their connecting trains. Some will simply leave the terminal, get in their cars and drive a short distance to a home in a "value priced" suburb. A few will walk to one of the several new high-rise apartment/home buildings with "panoramic views of the harbor and New York City". Less expensive living and less crime just a short ride away from their work.

The PATH train is empty and the cars are being swept for debris. The cars will accept riders back to the city in thirty minutes. Meanwhile a second train is loading at the PATH terminal in Manhattan. New bodies will be regurgitated onto the platform for track one at the Newark station in thirty minutes. This process will be repeated six times from four-thirty to seven p.m. Then the process becomes hourly until eleven.

Several uniformed workers are cleaning the men's and women's restrooms. Paper on the floor is the noticeable target of their efforts. There are also sinks that continue to run, toilets that were not flushed, and spills by the urinals in the men's rooms and commodes in the women's rooms. The scream of one male worker shatters the calm of the waiting.

Over the two-way radio, Billy Marshall calls, "Central, I have a body in men's room number two on the lower level. Repeat I have a body in men's room number two on the lower level. Call the police and send me help."

Billy stands in the door to prevent anyone but authorized personnel from entering. He has adopted the role of protector of the dead. After five agonizingly long minutes two uniformed policemen arrive to assume control of the crime scene. The victim is sitting slumped over in stall Number Three. Blood has cascaded from his sliced neck onto his shirt, jacket, pants, the floor, and an attaché case. He cannot be moved until the riding detectives and the ME have looked at him. Officer Bolton reaches inside the jacket at retrieves the man's wallet. His driver's license and other photo ID confirm that the deceased is Thomas Clarkton, a captain of special investigations for the Essex County Sherriff.

The arrival of the detectives and the ME's wagon necessitate the use of yellow tape that warns "Police Crime Scene Do Not Enter." The uniformed officers run the tape from the entrance to the rest room in a semi-circle around two support posts twenty feet from the door. Video cams are now recording the crime scene while reporters record the recording and seek to interview Billy, the two officers, and the detectives. Billy is confronted by a detective and admonished not to talk to anyone about anything. The officers know the proper procedure.

"Really bloody. Very personal. His watch and wallet were not taken. Ninety dollars in his wallet. Pinky ring remains on his left hand. It bears the insignia of a police force. Looks like NYPD."

"Okay, that's the obvious. What else can the ME tell us?"

"The killer was sending a message of some sort. His tongue was cut out. I'll know more when I get him in my lab. But for now, you guys have a real murder mystery on your hands. Let's bag him, get him on the gurney, and let me do my job."

"Officers, start a canvass of all people on both levels. Someone had to see something. We'll deal with the Transit Authority and their cops. This is a murder on our turf. I'll speak to the reporters."

"What can you tell us about the victim?"

"Male in his late forties. Robbery does not appear to be a motive."

"What is his name?"

"Not until we notify next of kin."

"How was he dressed?"

"Business casual. He had an attaché case."

"What was in the case?"

"Not sure. We open the case and review the contents back at the precinct. A formal announcement will be made around eight a.m. tomorrow. Thanks for your time."

The detectives must now begin the process of picking mites from a gnat. The thousand details that lead to an arrest and conviction. The next few days are critical.

Chapter 3

New York Ledger Friday, March 13, 2014
New Jersey Police Captain Slain
Captain Thomas Clarkton, a captain in the Essex County Sherriff's office, was found murdered in the Newark PATH terminal at 5:35 p.m. last evening. Captain Clarkton was a ten-year veteran of the Essex County Sheriff's office having served as a member of the NYPD SWAT team prior to joining the Essex County Sheriff. He is survived by his wife, Janet, and two children. No further details are available at this time.

Thomas Clarkton. Thomas Clarkton. Thomas Clarkton. *Why is that name familiar?* Tony can't recall, but it nags at his brain like a faded picture of a high school sweetheart. The best way to conjure the importance of the name and the person is to forget about thinking about it. The harder he thinks the deeper into the blind recesses of my mind the issue travels. The less he thinks about a conundrum, the greater the opportunity of the answer simply popping into his consciousness. It's like coffee percolating. The hunt for Thomas Clarkton will now go on sleep mode.

⁊⁊⁊

Fruiti di Mare the way Jessica prepares it is the children's favorite meal—chunks of grouper, lobster tail, shrimp, and mussels are steamed then blended into delicately seasoned and light cream sauce with crushed fennel seed. This mixture is folded into fettuccini and garnished with chopped fresh basil and Italian parsley. It is served family style from a seemingly bottomless dish at Jessica's station. The salad tonight is arugula, artichoke hearts, Greek olives, pecans and cherry tomatoes drizzled with homemade Balsamic vinaigrette dressing that sits at Jerry's station. Warm Italian bread is served with individual basil and extra virgin olive oil dishes. Doling out the bread is Melissa's responsibility.

The magnificent three attack the entrée as if they had not eaten for six months. They even use the bread to sop up the fettuccini sauce. They pick at the salad, until they see the raised eyebrow of their grandmother. The salad is eaten with slow measured chews. Their dinner is over in under twenty minutes—even with seconds.

"Thank you, Nana. The food was really good," is said in near unison.

"You're welcome, children. Now comes news update the time. Antonio, how are your grades?"

"Three As and two Bs, Nana. I'm playing on the JV baseball team. Catcher. I chose that position, because it is the most difficult and the most important on the squad. It's really tough. But I'm learning a lot. And it's fun."

"Tony and Lisa sitting in the tree, k-i-s-s-i-n-g, first comes love then comes marriage, then comes Lisa with a baby carriage."

"Cassandra. What are you saying?"

"Nana, she's just being a pest."

"Antonio, who is this Lisa?"

"She's a girl in my grade."

"Is she special to you?"

"Yes, Nana. She's smart, and we get along well. Plus, she is a terrific runner on the track team."

"Cassandra, teasing your brother is a time-honored way of telling him how much you love him. Does he tease you?"

"He calls me 'squirt' in front of my classmates. Just because I'm smaller than most of them, he thinks it's funny, but it's not funny."

"Do any of your classmates call you squirt?"

"No."

"If they did, they would have to answer to me."

"Antonio, that's good. Protecting your younger sister is what the older brother should do. But he should never tease her in front of others, because that gives them license to tease her. Understand?"

"Yes, Nana."

"Bartheleme, how is school?"

"Better grades than Antonio—all As. Plus, I have the lead in the Middle Division Spring Play, which will be given in May. I'm playing a dark and mysterious hero, who hides from his family, because of what they did to him when he was a child. The play was written by our drama teacher. I hope you'll come."

"Your grandfather and I wouldn't miss the event for all the world. We have a budding thespian in the family. How nice. Now to you, Cassandra. What are you doing that's extra special?"

"I'm working on a project for the science fair that will be held a week before the play."

"What is this project?"

"I'm trying to prove the theory of connectivity."

"And just what is the theory of connectivity?"

"Nene, you and Nana will have to come to the science fair and see."

Even at an early age, girls learn to flirt with the male of the species as method of control. Tony's daughter is no different.

"Now the three of you are excused. Your computer games are in den."

Tony and Melissa couldn't extract that much information from their children in an entire week. Jessica does it in less than fifteen minutes. Jessica could have given Torquemada lessons in truth extraction. Maybe she'll teach her techniques to Tony, before the children crash into the dangerous time of older teenage life.

Outside of the conversations between Melissa and her parents, Tony begins to drift back to Brooklyn and the once-a-month big Sunday family dinners. The feast rotated amongst three households—his parents, two sets of uncles and aunts, and a total of five children. At his home, they sat at a huge dinner table eating and talking about stuff. Just stuff. They all spoke at once. The volume of the conversations always became a din.

When the dinner was at his home, Tony was responsible for the table—open it and insert the middle extension, lay the table cloth, solid white and recently ironed by hand, the cloth was large enough to hang over the table's sides by six inches and the hang was checked by Mother, place the best china, silverware and glass ware at the eleven places. These meals were for the familia. All ate well. Plain, but well at whichever home they ate. Chicken, pork roast, or spaghetti and sausages with peppers and tomatoes were regular fare. Vegetables were always served from tureens with large serving spoons. The side dish was either steamed or baked with some kind of

tomato sauce. Dessert was ice cream or gelato and cookies from a local bakery.

At Tony's home, they all ate at the large table. At
Dante's or Sal's house, the children ate in the kitchen.
The children were responsible for clean up as supervised
by the woman of the household. The men went outside
for a smoke. It was smoking that killed his papa. Lefto-
vers were divided among the families. Nothing went to
waste. Tony had his first drink of alcohol, Chianti, when
he was fourteen. As the children grew, the parents spoke
of college. All five would go to college. This was or-
dained. Tony was the only one to get a degree from an
Ivy League university, Brown. The elder generation is
long since dead, and all but one cousin and Tony have
moved to the West Coast. Tony's cousin still lives in Al-
bany. At least he thinks so. He hasn't spoken to her in
years.

"Earth to Tony. Earth to Tony. Come in. Are you
there?"

"Sorry, I was just reminiscing about dinners at my
parents' home. Jessica, the meal was outstanding. Could
you teach Melissa how to cook like that?"

"Tony, I tried for so long and all of my teaching fell
on deaf ears. I finally gave up. My daughter seems the
think the kitchen's a foreign land filled with death and
destruction."

"Mother, how could you feel that way?"

"I have seen you among the pots, pans, and applianc-
es. What a tragedy."

"What can I do to help with clean up?"

"Tony, you're a dear. But this is my time to talk with
Melissa—you know, lady things. We'll offer the children
dessert in about thirty minutes. Now, you two male beasts
adjourn to Jerry's study. Melissa, bring the plates first.

I'll rinse them for the dishwasher. Do you know what that is?"

ↄ৯ে৩

"Tony, you can only imagine how much good these dinners are for Jessica. And me, of course. We want to spend as much time as possible with our grandchildren. Now, let me tell you what I know. Commander Vincent has been advised that Lieutenant Thomason will be the next CAT squad leader promoted to captain. Commander Vincent will advise Lieutenant Thomason of this fact, and suggest that it's in his best interest that he allows you to observe his investigation into the murder of Office Jamie Lanno. My guess is that Lieutenant Thomason will not welcome you with open arms, but his ego's so very large he'll quickly see the advantage of your observing. Just observing as an interested party. You'll have no investigative power. Just looking over Thomason's shoulder. And stay out of his way. Is that understood?"

"Yes, sir, and thank you. How soon can I call Lieutenant Thomason?"

"I suggest that you call him next Tuesday."

"That I will. Tuesday. And thanks again. I realize this cost a great deal of capital."

Tony could hear his heart beating at about eighty bpm and his blood pressure must have skyrocketed to 160 over 100. The excitement rivaled a child on December twenty-third.

He was back in the game, but without the baggage of being in the game. The perfect role for a consultant. Most important, he can help catch the bad guys. Yogi said it best—It's like déjà vu all over again. He will have to break this gently to Melissa.

"Okay, you two. Dessert and coffee in the dining room. The children are already enjoying their ice cream sundaes."

Jessica scoops vanilla ice cream into three dishes and places the toppings on a Lazy Susan in front of the children. Each can make their own delightfully rich finish to an equally rich dinner. The adults have Sorbet, coffee and cognac—a thirty-five-year-old treasure.

"Mother, Father, Tony and I have a request. Over the Memorial Day weekend we would like to go to both of our respective reunions. My reunion in New Haven is on Friday and Saturday and Tony's in Providence is on Sunday and Monday. We would like to leave Manhattan on Thursday around noon and drive north. Returning from Providence late Tuesday. We were hoping you two would watch the children over the extra-long weekend. You would stay at our place. Would you, please."

"Would we? We would love to spend the time with our grandchildren."

Jessica is almost beside herself with excitement. Tony can almost see her mind planning events and meals. Like a kid a Christmas. Jerry grins like a Cheshire cat.

"Great. Then that's settled, Mother. Thanks a ton. Over the next few weeks, we'll have lunch to discuss details. What a relief."

"Does this mean that we'll have newer and better parents for about five days?"

"Antonio, Nana and Nene will watch you like hawks. Your father and I will give them specific instructions about your eight p.m. bed time, household chores, and dietary restrictions like no pizza, no ice cream, no between meal snacks, and no cookies. Plus, we'll show them where we keep the paddles and leg irons."

"Mom, you're a phony tyrant."

"Don't worry, Antonio. One of a grandparent's core

responsibilities is to spoil the grandchild or grandchildren. Let them do what they want. This is our way of getting back at our child for all the anguish she caused us."

"Easy, guys.

"Nene. Would you like to learn how to play video games? I can teach you."

"Yes I would, Bartheleme. That would be grand. Sort of like new tricks for an old dog."

"Nana, would you teach me how to cook?"

"Cassandra, I'll do my best. Remember you're my daughter's child."

"And your granddaughter."

"Touché."

"Hey, team, it's almost nine. I'd better call Adolfo for our ride home. My guess, he'll be here in twenty minutes. Gather up anything you brought. Jessica, Jerry, the evening was, as always, most enjoyable. Let me add my thanks for helping us by being with the children over Memorial Day weekend. It means a lot to Melissa and me. Also the children will enjoy having us not around."

Adolfo arrives twenty-two minutes after Tony's call. Hugs and kisses all around at the door to the two-story house. Then the Sattill family piles into the car for the forty-minute trip from Queens to Manhattan.

"Okay, you guys. Get into your sleep clothes. TV until ten. Then lights out."

"Okay, Momma."

Tony goes into the boys' room. "Antonio, I would like to have chat. You're not in trouble. Okay?"

"Okay."

"I realize that at your age in today's world you're bombarded with messages and signals—particularly from girls, who mature earlier than boys. I'm not going to ask you what you know or what you have thought about. I just want you to understand, that when you become affectionate with a girl, 'no' means 'no' and 'yes' means 'no.' Think about what you may do and how that may affect your life, not to mention your emotions. Try to resist doing what everybody else does, and be your own man—understanding, and respectful, of girls and women. A brash action could ruin two lives. Does this make sense to you?"

"Yes."

"Do you have any questions? Remember what I told you—you can ask me anything; I'll tell you the truth; never lie to me; and whatever you may think of doing, I have done it, and it wasn't as much fun as I thought it was going to be. Any questions?"

"No. And don't worry about me and Lisa. We're just friends. Nothing else."

"I'll take a hug."

Tony gets a hug and wanders into the master bedroom suite.

"How was the talk?"

"I got more information from perps when I was on the force. I believe I was more uncomfortable than Antonio. But he's a great boy. He has his head on straight. Must have great parents."

"Well, the mother's great for sure. I'm not so sure about the boy's father. He's out of town a lot. Children, time for bed."

The zinger is not unfelt. She obviously doesn't want to nag, but she wants her feelings known.

Standing in front of the one-sixth of the double sink vanity, Tony flosses, rinses with mouthwash, and puts on a fresh T-shirt. Ready for a little late night reading and slumber. Thomas Clarkton. Now he knows! He was a wise-ass SWAT member, who shot off his mouth to anyone. Waaaay too macho. Always dressed as if he were going into battle somewhere in the Middle East. Carried a holstered Glock 9 and a .45 tucked into his pants at the small of his back. He loved his M-4. There were schoolboy rumors that he slept with it. Tony remembers him talking to the press when they raided the REACH Mission. He implied very clearly that his SWAT team was responsible for the success of the raid. He was quoted in the *Ledger* beneath the photo of his team escorting the bad guys into vans. He had two bad guys by the necks. The brass was not happy with his publicity-seeking performance. He took a five-day rip as a reminder to let others speak. And Tony got the promotion. Thomas Clarkton, dead before his time. He probably pissed off someone. RIP. Case closed. To bed.

⌘⌘⌘

Tuesday ten a.m. Time to call Lieutenant Thomason.

"Lieutenant, this is Captain Tony Sattill. I was wondering if you had a few minutes today to discuss a request."

"Retired Captain Sattill, who's no longer with the NYPD, what kind of request?"

"Lieutenant, I'm aware that you caught the murder of Jamie Lanno. I know that you know she was a team member of mine. I would deeply appreciate the opportunity to observe your investigation. I will not interfere with it. I just want to be privy to what you know and what you're doing. I won't get in your way. I just want to observe."

"Retired Captain Sattill, we both know that I have been advised to allow you in as an observer. So let's cut the crap. I'll allow you to access the file electronically, assuming you have clearance. No need for you to trek all the way out to the slum of Queens from your penthouse in Manhattan."

"Lieutenant, I'm more than willing to come to your precinct so I can see firsthand what you have, not just what's in the reports. I can be there in an hour, if that's okay with you?"

"That'll be fine. If, for some strange reason, I'm not here when you arrive, just ask the desk sergeant to take you the conference room. I may be out of the precinct working on a case. All of our information will be there. Okay?"

"Many thanks."

CLICK

He acted just as Tony thought he would. Tony had pissed on his parade. He knew that he knew that he knew. He had no choice. His control over the case could be compromised if he did not let Tony in, and he feared his control over the case could be comprised by Tony. For his ego, this was a possible lose-lose situation. If he just kept quiet, swallowed his ego, and played nice, he would get the promotion he passionately sought, whether he deserved it or not. And Tony thought he did not.

The trek to Precinct Number Twelve on Queens Boulevard requires two subway lines and takes a little more than an hour. No Adolfo today. Subway travel is the great equalizer. At the precinct, the desk sergeant asks for my ID. Tony tins his way in. He gets a rookie to take him to the conference room on the second floor, because—shock of shocks—Lieutenant Thomason is not in the building.

Neatly arranged around the table are the files and hard evidence that sum up the last hours of his friend, Jamie Lanno's life. This once vibrant, intelligent, and fiercely effective woman has been reduced to paper and scraps of cloth inside polyethylene bags.

Begin with the ME's report. Multiple blunt force traumas to the head. The first would have stunned her.

The second and third killed her and traumas four through six were a very ugly message that this was personal. The cut in her throat was left to right, indicating the assailant was right handed. The angle of the cut indicated that it was made when Officer Lanno was lying face down on the concrete. She was already dead. Her slacks and panties were found around her ankles. The surgery to her clitoris was closer to amateurish than professional. The perp appears to have had some vague knowledge of surgery. No sign of sexual assault. Stomach contents consisted of a ham and cheese sandwich, Diet Coke, and Starburst candy. Estimated TOD was between four to six hours before discovery of the body.

Enough!

Jamie's blouse and pants are in one bag. Her under garments were in another. A third bag contained her watch, a small heart on a thin necklace, a wedding ring, her wallet with all the appropriate cards and some bills, a ChapStick, and eighty-seven cents in change. Jamie always had and used her ChapStick. She used to complain that the New York City air-dried her lips, the detective reports.

Canvass of the immediate area turned up nothing. Scuff marks indicate that Officer Lanno was partially carried and partially dragged into the stairwell. This could indicate multiple perps. No perp clues. Workers at the airport, who were questioned, knew nothing and saw no one of a suspicious nature. Several remarked that it would have been impossible to enter the stairwell without setting off the emergency alarm unless the individual knew the security code. It could have been a fellow worker—maintenance, sanitation, or security. Maybe a vendor employee. Maybe even one of the workers questioned. There were 129 workers on duty during the hours of Officer

Lanno's visit to the airport. Of these, twenty-six were assigned to airside A.

Damn, Tony realizes that he must have walked right by where she lay. Of the twenty-six, interviews were conducted during the first twenty-four hours with twenty-four workers and vendors. The remaining two were interviewed a day later. Names, addresses, telephone numbers and employee badge numbers are listed in order of interview.

Cherie Benedetti, Jamie's wife, heard the news and went into a rage. She calmed down and stated that she had no idea who would do this to her husband. After seventy-two hours the body will be released to Ms. Benedetti, for burial.

A request was made to the Sex Crimes Unit for Jamie's case files and histories. A huge folder contains the sum of her work at the unit plus the observations of her captain. The detectives under Thomason divided up the files, initialed what they took, and provided information as they garnered it on each case. Nothing truly out of the ordinary. *Except...*

All of the forms in all of the folders are copies of originals. Why were there no originals? Not even the ME's report was an original. The signature didn't smear when moistened. *Thomason is playing games. Hiding something to trip me up. That putz.* Tony takes pictures on his cell phone of all the pertinent reports and sends the pictures to his home computer for further review. Simultaneously send the virtual paperwork to Brendan and Chris for their review. Back to the subway and home.

Chapter 4

"Captain, what do you make of the information? It seems light for someone who's bucking for a promotion. Where are the detailed statements of those interviewed? All we see here are two-three lines. Just responses. No interpretation of the responses. No list of questions. How do we know each person was asked the same questions? This is very shoddy."

"Brendan, what you can't see is that all the files are dupes of originals. Copies indicate to me that something or some reports are missing. I have to tactfully inquire of Lieutenant Thomason about the reason for this situation. Chris, what can you add?"

"I spoke to my contact in sex crimes. He said that Thomason made a request for open files or those closed within the past two years. He purposefully limited the scope of his investigation. I requested copies of all her files including those sent to Thomason. This may give us some clue about his investigation. I'll let you know what I find when I compare what Thomason supplied and what my pals supplied. Captain, I have to jump off now. I'll stay in touch. We can't forget Jamie."

❦

Tony's agent calls with requests for seminars from police departments in Baltimore, Dallas, Denver, Philadelphia, and Lancaster, PA. The Philly, Baltimore, and Lancaster events can be done on a single three-day trip. Drive to Baltimore, then Lancaster, then Philly. Then home. She will get more information about the issues facing each city, and plan dates for two or three weeks from now. The Denver-Dallas trip can happen after the reunions. Tony must discuss it with Melissa. *Oh, joy!*

❦

"Captain, this is Chris. From going over the files, I found out that Thomason, by limiting Jamie's files to the last two years, conveniently omitted two files that involved a link between Manhattan and Queens Sex Crimes units. I also discovered that the files he did review were not sanitized for your eyes and they offer no leads. The perps are in jail or dead. The two he omitted with the Queens connection dealt with kiddy porn and park stalking. Complaints by several mothers and grade school teachers. But no touching and no molestation were reported. Because of the amount and brutal type of kiddy porn on the home computers, the two got eight to ten. Remember that these are separate, non-connected cases that occurred in different areas of Queens.

"The two perps with the Queens connection are alive and living in Jackson Heights. They served at different facilities and have different homes addresses. They served their time and make regular visits to their different and respective POs. I want to check with their POs, but I'll bet they're clean. The net of all this is that unless I can dig up something on the two perps from Queens, Jamie's files don't look like a fertile ground for further exploration. I looked at her open cases. They're all domestic. She had just opened three cases, so I doubt there could be any angry dads. But I'll double check with her supervisor."

"Great. I have to talk to Thomason about why he provided abridged copies of files. I still think he's trying to hide something."

"Be careful, Captain, tact was never your strength. You don't want the door slammed in your face."

"I'll be a polite as a debutant."

Next call is to Brendan to see if he discerned anything about the copied files.

"Captain, I noticed a few glitches in the material. The ME's report is missing what appears to be page three. Although page two ends with a complete sentence, the inference to be drawn from the sentence is that there is more to be said. Can you open your files?"

"Give me a second. Got it."

"See the line that deals with TOD? Estimated TOD was between four to six hours before discovery of the body."

"Got it."

"My friend who works with the Manhattan ME told me that to support the TOD statement there should have been some statement of body rigor, but there was none. There should have been a statement of liver temp, but there was none. There should have been some statement about blood loss, but there was none. My friend concludes this indicates omission. She knows the Queens ME and will vouch for her integrity. I think that Thomason is hiding something."

"Great catch, Brendan."

"There's more. I think the questioning of the airport workers and vendors was superficial at best and damn shoddy at worst. The answers seem to be too similar—too vague. I cannot believe that no one saw two men herding a lurching, semi-conscious Jamie toward the stairwell from the aisle between the gates. I cannot believe that no one heard the alarm as the exit door was opened. Nor, can I believe no one saw two men shove Jamie into the stairwell. But what I can believe is that the men who killed and mutilated her wore worker uniforms to blend in with the other workers. The worker uniforms are universal gray with no insignia. And they learned the security code to the exit door. Here's how. They saw someone else enter the code and memorized it from watching the other employee press specific buttons on the key box. They had followed Jamie that day and seized the opportunity to attack at the airport. Captain, there are too many unanswered questions. Why Jamie? How long were they following her? Why now? Who are they? What's their connection to Jamie? "

"Brendan, keep digging. I think you're on to something—maybe many things. Two perps following her for a while. Call me when you learn something new. I need to delicately press these files issues with Thomason today."

"Be diplomatic, Captain. We don't want to be locked out."

ↄ〇ↄ

Baseball in the early spring is truly a harbinger of summer's pastoral pastime. Antonio looks like he weighs a buck eighty-five with all his gear. The Day School JV team is playing University Prep School's JVs. As Tony looks around, he is one of four adult males in the stands. The balance of the sparse crowd is made up of coeds and buddies. It is nippy, but sunny. No wind. Antonio has a hectic first three innings, as the pitcher learns to throw the ball somewhere near the plate. A lot of scrambling left and right, and digging the bouncing ball out of the dirt. Their pitcher is no better.

In the fourth inning Antonio throws out a base runner trying to steal second. The other coach is testing the catcher. Antonio's looks like a lob, but the runner is slow, so all's well that ends with a put out. In the fifth inning, Antonio hits a fly into the right-center gap that rolls to the fence. He makes it to second huffing and puffing. The next batter hits a fly to deep right, and Antonio lumbers onto third. The number seven batter strokes a clean single to left and Antonio scores. Great jubilation.

University Prep goes down in order in the top of the sixth and final inning. The Day School is now two and two. Tony whistles and Antonio acknowledges his father's presence by lifting his mitt into the air, but never looking toward the stands. That would be way too childish.

∽∾∽

"Lieutenant Thomason, this is Tony Sattill. I had a chance to review the files you left out for me the other day, and I was wondering if you have some time to discuss my observations?"

"Not today, retired Captain Sattill. But I can fit you in tomorrow at seven a.m. in my office, if that is not inconvenient."

"Thanks. That would be great. See you tomorrow then."

Asshole. He is deliberately making it difficult for me. But truth will prevail. If for no other reason than for Jamie.

∽∾∽

Tony's agent calls back with confirmed dates—Baltimore on the fifth, Lancaster on the sixth and Philadelphia on the seventh—Monday, Tuesday, Wednesday. Fly into Baltimore, speak on Monday, then drive to Lancaster that night, stay one night, and talk the next day. Then drive to Philly for the day. Exhausted, fly home Wednesday evening. Easy peasy. She will e-mail the particulars about each PD; issues, names, addresses, numbers. She noted that there were serial crimes in each city. Made a passing comment about illegal buggy races, extortion, protection, and gambling by the Amish Mafia. Now to break the news to Melissa.

"I'm not crazy about your trips, but you'll be gone for only three days and you'll be in the same time zone. Promise you'll call each night. I miss your voice. Just hearing your voice is almost like being with you. I really miss being with you. Touching you and being touched by you. I want to us to be able to casually share the events of each day with our partner. Plus, the darlings can be a handful, when they know the dad is not around. When you call I will ask you to speak to them about your day. Very casually. Do you think that's weird?"

"No, sweetie, what you feel is important to me. And I love you even more when we can share time, even if that time is telephone time."

Deep sleep was preceded by aggressive affection and the exchange of bodily fluids. Melissa is very good at that. The alarm rang much too early. Shower, shave, dress, and down to the subway for my rush hour ride to Queens.

"Lieutenant, I appreciate you taking time from your busy day to listen to my observations."

"Not a problem. Always willing to help a retired civilian. Now what have you observed?"

"I noticed the thorough and comprehensive interrogation of the various possible witnesses. But I wondered if you spoke to anybody who was at the taxi stand that evening? If Officer Lanno was forced into the stairwell, it may have required two men. I doubt one man alone could have overpowered her. And, I doubt that two men were waiting for her at the airport. Therefore, these two men had to follow her to the airport. Since she took a cab to the airport, they too, had to take a cab. Maybe a cabby remembers them. Maybe the dispatcher remembers two men together entering the airport about the same time that Office Lanno entered. Just an observation."

"That is a very interesting line of reasoning. When they have the time, I'll have my men canvass the taxis and speak to the dispatcher. Is there anything else?"

"Now that you ask, yes there is. I seemed to have missed a page in the MEs report dealing with rigor, liver temp, and blood loss."

"I'll get that for you."

"And one more item. The pages in the files were copies of originals. Is there any reason the originals were not made available for my review?"

"There must have been an administrative error. We do keep originals in the file folders and save copies electronically. I'll double-check the files to see what went wrong. Is that it?"

"I guess so for now."

"Well I have some comments for you. Tell your Manhattan ME to keep his hands off my case. Doesn't he have enough work on his tables? Why go looking for work and the trouble of interfering with an on-going investigation? Also, I know your buddy, Lieutenant Chris Wills, has been digging into Lieutenant Lanno's files. He asked for and received the same files that I did. It's almost like he was looking over my shoulder. Just like you are. Tell him to stop, and I won't push to have him brought up on the charge of interference."

"Let me tell you what I know," Tony snarled. "Your work so far on this case has been shoddy, at best. It's almost as if you don't care, because you know you're next in line. Well, my good buddy, if my report of your handling of this case were to make it to One PP, your chances of promotion would swirl the porcelain bowl. So here's what we're going to do. You're going to interview the taxi drivers and the dispatcher to find out whom, if anybody, followed Lieutenant Lanno into the airport. I suspect that there were two people who took a particular interest in Jamie. Second, you'll make available to me the complete and original files—all of them, not just your sanitized versions. And three, your men will talk to two sex offenders who were in Lieutenant Lanno's files before your arbitrary two-year cut off. You can access their case files, just like I did. They live in your borough. And after all this, we'll reconvene…say in three days. In your office at ten. Is that understood?"

"You bastard."

"Actually, I'm not a bastard. But I can be a prick. I'd rather be your supporter. Fair enough? You can be a hero or a goat. I can use the carrot or the stick. Your call."

"I'll see you in three days. Now get out the fuck out of my office and my precinct."

The ride home was enjoyable. Tony is back at it.

ჭჳჭ

"Chris, Brendan, let me bring you up to speed."

During the next ten minutes, Tony lays out the present set of circumstances, his plan and his possible course of action.

"So, gentlemen, what I learn in a few days will direct where we go with our parallel investigation. I appreciate your work and the speed with which it was conducted. Your assistance will not go unnoticed at One PP. I'll stay in touch."

৩৩৩৩

Back to the subway and the Queens precinct of Lieutenant Thomason.

"Good morning, Sergeant. I'm here to see Lieutenant Thomason. Allow me to sign in while you call upstairs."

Tony is waved through and nearly bounds up the stairs to Thomason's office.

"Good morning, Lieutenant, let's get right to it. What have you learned?"

"Here's the information we were able to gather since your last visit. We spoke to the dispatcher and he could not recall your Lieutenant Lanno or anyone following her. But the security cameras spotted her—" Thomason plays the disc. "See her get out of a cab. Now watch as two black men exit their cab immediately after her. Notice they're wearing gray pants and shirts. Very nondescript. Plus, they have their plain black ball caps pulled down over their foreheads to hide their faces from the camera. We can follow Lieutenant Lanno and the two men with the security cameras along the way to the gates. As they go up the stairs and head toward the airside gates they are about thirty feet behind Lieutenant Lanno. Obviously stalking her.

"The men do not go through security, but they watch to see which gate the lieutenant selects. The two men turn around and go into the restroom on the main floor. They exit about ten minutes later in airport workers coveralls, complete with ID badges. They pass through security with no problem and hover near Gate B-24. The same gate as your lieutenant. There is almost no one at or near the gate at this time. Lieutenant Lanno heads to the ladies' room. We're able to follow her using the security cameras in sequence along the passage way. The two phony workers hover near the restroom. See, they do not look up. Obviously, they know about the surveillance cameras, and they're avoiding detection.

"When Lanno leaves the rest room and begins to head to her gate, the two men encase her—one in front and one behind. When the three of them get next to the stairwell, the perp behind Lanno hits her on the back of the head. At the same time, the perp in front of Lanno turns to catch her. To keep her from falling. The man that hit her now punches in a pass code to open the door to the stairwell so as not to set off the alarm. Then the two of men escort her through the open door, which closes rapidly behind them. All of this happened in about five seconds. The security camera shows that none of the few civilians in the aisle took notice of what was happening. In eight minutes, the stairwell door opens and the two perps exit. They walk nonchalantly to the same men's room they entered before the abduction and murder. In three minutes, they exit the men's room carrying a duffle bag, most likely filled with their phony coveralls.

"Now watch the next part of the tape. The two guys still hide their faces with ball caps. They exit to the taxi stand and walk directly to the third cab in line. This is a big No-No. Obviously, this cab was important to them. We got the external cab number and the license plate. We learned it had been stolen that day and was found burned to a crisp in New Jersey. We checked with the Essex County Sheriff's office to see if there was any additional information on the cab or the vehicle in which they left after they torched the cab. Essex County told us there was too much traffic—too many tire tracks—in the area to determine what happened to the cab riders."

"Nice work, Thomason. Is there any way we can see who the two men are?"

"We enlarged what little we saw of their faces. As you can see the faces are very boney, you could say angular, and the guys are very black."

A chill hit Tony like a Nordic blast. This type of facial structure and coloring was all he saw at the REACH Mission fifteen years ago. What the fuck is happening? Is history repeating itself? Sweat is dripping down the back of his neck. Is it cold or has did his skin chill? There is a clammy dread permeating his body and the knot in his stomach makes sitting upright difficult. As he blinks he senses flashes of the Mission, being shot, Jimmie's death, and his first born.

"I'll issue an APB for the two men, but I don't hold out much hope of finding them. They took a lot of care to conceal their identities. Hell, I'll bet they're not even in the area any longer."

"I would appreciate copies of the enlarged photos. I want to study them."

"Sure thing. We checked out the two pervs who Officer Lanno arrested. The two appear to have straightened out their lives, and they have rock solid alibis for the time when Lanno was at the airport. Sorry, no help there."

"You did good work. Tied up loose ends. I think the two black men are your only avenue. I won't need the complete files. I'm confident they won't shed any new light on the events. Again thanks for your good work. Stay at it."

All the way back to Manhattan, Tony stares at the blurry surveillance photos of Jamie's killers, and tries to connect them to the Mission case of fifteen years ago.

ⁿⁿ

"So that's what I know. Chris? Brendan? Can either of you determine the whereabouts of the perps we put away as part of the raid on the REACH Mission? I thought most of them got fifteen to twenty years. If that's accurate, it is possible some of them were let out on the streets after twelve years. We need to find them. I'll scan the blurry surveillance photos Lieutenant Thomason gave me and send them to you both so you can match the faces with any recent parolees. Better go back four years to be sure. If these two were part of the Mission gang, their motive for killing Jamie might have something to do with her handling of their queen. She was pretty rough on the bitch. Call me as soon as you find something."

"Captain, let me ask how you got so much from Thomason, when he showed us so little last week."

"The power of positive persuasion. He desperately wants to be promoted to captain. I simply showed him the fastest avenue to that goal. Honesty works wonders."

ⁿⁿ

"Captain, Chris and I found some interesting information about the perps from the Mission we put away fifteen years ago. There were a total of sixteen males and four females, excluding the queen. Disregarding the females for the time being, we learned that of the sixteen males, twelve are alive today. Their distribution was nationwide. Of these twelve, two went to Sing Sing, two went to Iowa State Prison at Amoroso, two went to Florida State prison at Stark, and two went to New Mexico State prison outside of Taos, two went to Attica in upstate, and two went to Alabama State prison at Holman. Of these twelve, eight are still incarcerated. The eight who remain in prison have had various scrapes with authorities and other inmates and will serve out their full twenty. Four were paroled between two and three years ago. These four were all incarcerated in New York—either at Sing Sing or Attica.”

“Chris did some further digging and learned that all four are here in the metro area, two in New Jersey and two in the Bronx. Chris got the names of PO’s for all four, and he reached out to them. He asked the PO’s to contact me. One of the PO’s called me. By the way, Chris is going on a well-deserved vacation to Costa Rica, and will be gone for a week, and he didn’t want to slow up our work. Besides, my case load is light, and I would love to nail the bastards who hurt Jamie.”

“I cross checked the blurry surveillance photos with mug shots of the four who are in the area, and I think we have a match. It’s tough to be positive, but I’m leaning strongly to confirming a resemblance.”

“Great work, you guys. What are the names of the four in our area?”

“Their American names they use now are Benny Radle, David Ellis, Wilson Abraham, and Ernest Davis. Their names at the Mission and at their trial were Betoto Magname, Ugata Nmbata, Dekena Rbille, and Nuta Breata. I may have mispronounced some of the names. Too many consonants and not enough well-placed vowels.”

“Who do you think are in the surveillance photos?”

“The two look like David Ellis and Wilson Abraham. They both have the same PO and they live in the Bronx. The other two live in New Jersey.”

“Do you have addresses for the two in the Bronx?

“Yes, I do. But you’re not going there without me. Remember you’re a civilian. I’m the law enforcement officer, and they're on my turf. When would you like to pay a call on these guys?"

"I'll meet you at your precinct at six-thirty tomorrow morning. I want to get to them before they disappear into the faceless mass that is the city."

"They both missed their last appointments with their PO a week ago. So it looks like disappearance is on their agenda. One last interesting point. They live around the corner from each other. How very convenient."

Tony has a Glock 9 and a Colt .32. Home protection weapons. The Glock he kept from his days on the force. The .32 he purchased for Melissa. She learned to shoot, and is not afraid to protect herself and her family with it. Handling the Glock makes him almost giddy. He'll take one extra clip. He's back at it. Some real excitement has just revved up his life. With his captain's badge and department-issued Kevlar vest, he is ready. Not sure he was supposed to keep the vest. But what the hell. What they say is true. To be a good cop, you have to be an adrenalin junky. The fear of the unknown—the hunt—has to get all your organs working at max speed. When the hunt is over and the bad guys are in jail or dead, the adrenalin junky suffers a crash worse than post coital depression. And if the adrenalin is not exploited for a long period of time, life for the junky slows to a pace slower than that of an octogenarian. Long gaps between adrenalin rushes can lead to suicide of the junky. Why live if there is nothing to live for?

Chapter 5

The Day School Theater is dark except for stage lights. Tony enters quietly and slides into an aisle seat in the second to last row. The actors hold script folders and read as they stand in their assigned places. No action yet. Tony hears Bartheleme whispering, yet trying to keep his voice deep as if he were a dark and mysterious hero. There are four people center stage while Bartheleme is in the back ground, stage left. The stage hands are busy building and painting the appropriate scenery. The flurry of activity is somewhat noisy, and they are called out by the director. He immediately turns his attention to the actors on stage, and urges them to speak up, but not to yell. He commands more feeling and emotion as he lays out the scene's back story.

He urges Bartheleme to stand half way between the bright lights of stage front and the darkness of the shadows as if he were caught between two worlds—one of their making and one of his making. Tony listens to Bartheleme whisper his tale of life's cruelty, family betrayal, and lost love. Very heavy for a young teen. Upon the completion of Bartheleme's soliloquy, Tony applauds. The sound of one man clapping reverberates throughout the empty theater. Both the director and Bartheleme peer into the darkness to spot the intruder. The director scowls, but Bartheleme waves and bows as Tony exits theater right.

☙❧

"I have to leave the house before six tomorrow morning."

"Why so early?"

"Brendan and I have a lead on those involved in Jamie's killing, and we want to talk to two guys before they go to work."

"Are you going as Tony Sattill or Captain Sattill?"

"Just as Tony—as back up for Brendan. He has the authority. I'm just an observer."

"But, just in case there's trouble, you'll be taking your gun and vest, right?"

"Just for protection. If these guys are the guys who killed Jamie, we know they're violent. Hopefully, our early arrival will take them by surprise and make them willing to talk with us. Because they're on parole, they must talk to the police if asked to do so."

"Jesus, Tony. You're going to suit up for war. Like old times. Kick in a few doors. Jump on the bad guys. Then strong arm them into a confession."

"You're way off base. I have no standing or authority. I'll be nothing more than back-up."

"For your family's sake, I hope that's all. How do you plan to get from here to Brendan's in your battle gear? Subway? Bus? Walk?"

"Taxi."

"How ludicrous. A cop goes to battle in a taxi. Hollywood would do that for comedic relief."

"I told you I won't be a combatant. I'll be carrying my piece, shield, and vest in a duffle bag so that I can make ready at Brendan's precinct. Besides, he told me these guys missed their last appointment with their PO. So there is a good chance, they're not even at home. Now come here."

⌘

"Jack, I'm taking the dogs for their walk. Be back in about thirty minutes."

Down to the lobby and out the door, the Pulik are well behaved. Jack and Joan Mussleman spent a substantial amount of money buying and learning to properly handle the two Hungarian sheep herding dogs. Pulik are special. No one knows of a connection to any other breed. There are stories of sheep herders swapping ten sheep for a single Puli puppy. The dogs don't herd like other herding canines. They run across the back of the flock to get to the strategic side. They simply know what side of the flock is the steering side. And, they rarely bark at the flock. They herd with their presence. The sheep seem to know to obey the visual commands of a Puli. They are very protective of their living environment and their masters. They will bark or growl at strangers, whom they sense may be a threat, but they will not attack the stranger.

Once the woman and beasts are on the sidewalk, Joan unhooks the leads from the collars. The Pulik walk briskly to the corner and wait for her. She has wondered aloud about who walks whom? At the green light and with a paucity of traffic, Joan commands that they run. And run, they do—right to the walk way leading into the park. There they wait again for the human. Upon her arrival, the three of them enter. The dogs trot to trees and to the grass near a lamp. Joan dutifully picks up their deposits, as they sprint away to play their favorite game of chase.

At eleven-thirty p.m., Jack Mussleman calls his wife on the cell phone. There is no answer. The next call is to the police.

New York Ledger Tuesday, March 28, 2014
DA Murdered in Park
Executive Assistant District Attorney, Joan Mussleman was found murdered in Central Park at 12:05 a.m. today. She was found slumped over on a park bench. There were no witnesses. Two dogs were found beside the bench. Mrs. Mussleman's husband, Jack stated that his wife routinely took the couple's dogs into the park for a walk. The NYPD has established a tip line, 212-599-3497 for any information about the murder. All calls will be kept confidential. The City is offering $50,000 reward for information leading to the capture of the person or persons who murdered DA Mussleman.

ೞೞ

"Captain, did you see who got murdered last night? Joan Mussleman, the executive assistant DA. Killed in the park while walking her dogs."

"Who is she, other than a suit?"

"Her maiden name was Kemp. She was ADA, Joan Kemp. The one who facilitated the raid on the Mission and the arrest of the perps—large and small—in the case."

"Oh, yeah, I remember now. She married the hedge fund manager, who made everybody very rich. That's a shame. She was smart, tough, and good looking. How did she die?"

"She was murdered in Central Park, while walking her dogs. That's what the public knows. We know her throat was slit and her tongue was cut out. Very bloody. Some sort of message. The department is working with the DA's office in the review of her open cases and those closed within the past five years."

"Jesus. Who among us is safe? Now where do we go first?'

"David Ellis lives at twelve forty-seven Thirty-Fourth Street and Wilson Abraham lives at three thirty-eight One Hundred Twenty-Second Avenue. Right around the corner. Let's hit Ellis first. Suit up old timer."

The vest is a little snug around the belly and the Glock feels heavier than Tony remembered. Arrive at the Ellis address in about ten minutes. Six-story building that has seen many better days. Still clean and no broken windows. They buzz the super.

"Waddaya want?"

"I'm Lieutenant McLaughlin and this is Captain Sattill. We're here to speak to Mr. David Ellis. Please let us in and accompany us to his apartment."

"Ellis, eh. Haven't seen that guy for two weeks. He owes rent for that time."

"What is his apartment number?"

"He rented three-B."

"Come with us. We'll need you to open his door."

The banging is less than cordial. Hopefully, it will get the resident's attention.

"David Ellis, this is the NYPD. We want to talk to you."

Silence from inside. Three more fist bangs.

"David Ellis, this is the NYPD. Please open the door. We want to talk to you."

Silence from inside.

"Okay, use your key, and unlock the door. Then step aside and let us enter. Stay in the hall far behind us. David Ellis, we're coming into your apartment. Just relax. We only want to talk."

Brendan's words echo within the empty space.

The two rooms have been vacated. Sheets are still on the bed, and dirty dishes sit in the kitchen sink. Tony and Brendan have come up empty. They search for anything that would be a clue as to where Ellis was headed when he bolted. Nada.

"Captain, I was afraid of this dead end. My guess is that we'll find the same nothing at Abraham's apartment. If that's so, we'll have to go back to the precinct and try to make sense of what we know."

"Who's gonna pay me for the two weeks he owes? When can I rent this place?"

"Send the bill to the mayor. As soon as we leave."

Tony and Brendan walk to Wilson Abraham's apartment just around the corner. There they see a repeat of what they saw in Ellis's place. The ride back to the precinct is quiet. Both men are deep in thought.

"Here's what we know. Jamie was killed by two guys who we think were integral to the Mission case. She handled the arrests of the three harpies that ran the money-laundering, weapons-buying exploitation of the helpless was the scheme, and she was not very gentle in her treatment of the women. Jamie was sexually mutilated. They destroyed her womanhood. And the two guys who murdered her have disappeared. Joan Mussleman was the voice of the people that put the bad guys away for a long time, and she was just murdered. Mussleman had her throat slit and her tongue cut out. The ways in which the two women were murdered are messages. The perps are seeking literal and symbolic revenge for the evil wrought by the two women. Clarkton was an arrogant asshole who claimed the credit for the raid and downfall of the Mission. And he was murdered. I'll bet his tongue was cut out, too."

"Way ahead of you, Captain. I'll call the Essex County PO to see if Benny Radle and Ernest Davis have missed their most recent meetings. More than likely, they have. Then I'll contact the Essex County Sheriff and suggest, in the spirit of cooperation, someone go to the most recent addresses of the two. If they've moved, we have another connector. I'll also contact the Newark PD to see if they'll give me detailed information about Clarkton's murder. If his tongue was cut out, we have a trifecta. Not sure what we do about it, but we'll think of something."

Tony nodded. "In the meantime, be careful. It's possible that that anyone connected to the Mission raid is not safe. The sooner we have evidence that the three murders are connected, the sooner we can go to One PP for protection and more feet on the street to catch these assholes."

"Be safe. Protect your family. I'll sleep at the precinct, until we have a way to resolve this situation."

All the way home, Tony played out various scenarios, all starting with what if…

ఴఴఴ

"Captain, we have the trifecta. The two parolees in Jersey are nowhere to be found, and Clarkton had his throat slit and his tongue cut out. What do we do now?"

"Brendan, four steps. First, you develop a list of all those connected with the Mission case from arrest through trial. Focus primarily on those, who were visible or outspoken. Make sure you get the jurors' particulars. Get that to me yesterday. Second, you and Chris must find some way to become invisible. No routines. No regular events. Maybe move into a hotel for a while. Third, I have to find a way to convince One PP and the feds that this is really happening. I need the list of names for my presentation. And last but not least, we need to review the prison records of the four skels. Who were they close with? What mail and telephone messages they sent and received? Who visited them? Maybe this will tell us where they are?"

"Got it. Chris is back. I'll fill him in and divide the work load so we can have the list to you by tomorrow noon."

The cold wave of fear and angst rolled over Tony as he called his father-in-law, Jerry.

"The murder of Jamie is just a hint of things to come. I'm fairly sure we have links between the murders of Joan Mussleman, Office Clarkton over in New Jersey, Jamie and four of those who went to jail as a result of our raid fifteen years ago. These four were paroled into the Bronx and Northern New Jersey. Jerry, I'll inform Lieutenant Thomason of our findings as they pertain to his case of Jamie's murder, and walk him through the expanded scenario. I need a rabbi at One PP before this thing becomes a mass execution. I don't know how fast the clock is ticking, but I must assume time is of the essence. Can you help me?"

"Jesus, Tony, that's a lot to absorb in such a short time. How sure are you about the links?"

"Ninety percent."

"That's good enough for me. I recommend you call Commander Terry Vincent. I'll bet he would love to get his bureaucratic hands deep into the mud. Protecting the civil servants who serve the public would look very good on a plaque the NYPD will give him. Plus, if memory serves me, he has connections with various federally initialed agencies. And you'll need this connection. The trial was state level for the soldiers and then at the federal level for the three top dogs—Razdarovich, Linder, and Makeda. I have a personal question. How safe is your family?"

"For now, they're safe, because I was out of the spotlight. But I'll request police security for all the people associated with the case—including Chris, Brendan, and my family. Sorry for being abrupt, but I want to call Thomason and Vincent. Thanks for your help. I'll keep you in the loop."

Thomason was not pleased about Tony's extracurricular work, but he was pleased by the prospect of being on the ground floor of an extensive investigation. He could see the smiles and captain's bars. What he doesn't understand is that, from here on out, Thomason and his discovery will be just a notation of the investigations genesis.

"Commander Vincent, this is Captain Sattill. First, I want to thank you for encouraging Lieutenant Thomason to let me be an observer during his investigation. We worked well together, and he opened my eyes to some interesting facets of his work. I was wondering if you had about an hour today or tomorrow to discuss some interesting findings. I've already discussed them with Thomason. I need your sage counsel as to the next steps"

"Let me look at my calendar. Yes, I can see you today at four. Can you be here then?"

"Yes, I can, and thank you."

The list will have to be sent tomorrow.

His calendar. Who does he think he is kidding? He spends his day reviewing his pension, setting lunches, and going to ceremonial openings.

His calendar, indeed

ѽ

Thanks for seeing me on such short notice. What I want to discuss are the murders of Lieutenant Jamie Lanno, Executive Assistant District Attorney Joan Mussleman, and Captain Thomas Clarkton of the Essex County Sheriff's Office in New Jersey. Although they may seem far afield, I believe there's a dangerous link connecting the three with four recently paroled men who were involved in the Mission raid, arrests, and trial fifteen years ago. Let me layout the details."

It takes about forty-five minutes to review the assumptions and details with Commander Vincent. He raised some good and some not good questions which were interruptions during the process. As Tony was coming to the end of his presentation, Vincent glanced several times at his watch. The train home was beginning to take priority over Tony's case.

"Well, you present an interesting scenario. If you turn over all your information and assumptions to the department, I'm sure we'll take it under advisement."

"That's not what I had in mind, sir."

"What do you expect the department to do about your assumptions?"

"I expect the NYPD to let me back in for the resolution of this case. Hell, my team started the whole mess fifteen years ago, now one of my team, as well as two others associated with the case, has been murdered. I think I can help drive the investigation without stepping on too many toes."

"Mister Sattill, you're a retired captain. I stress retired. You're no longer under the auspices of the police department because your standing in the community is that of an ordinary civilian. To let you back in, as you say, would set a bad precedent. The precedent is that, if a civilian has knowledge of a crime, he or she can request a very detailed ride-along during the investigation. We can't have that, now can we?"

"With all due respect, I have way more skin in the game than an average civilian, plus I know these bastards. They and their murders are an extension of the case my team closed. If the facts are accurate, and they are, and if my assumptions are on target, and I firmly believe they are, numerous other people involved with closing the Mission case could be in grave danger. I'll have the complete list of those involved at the state and federal levels for you tomorrow. Then, I'd like to discuss appropriate next steps. Is that okay with you?"

"By numerous other people, do you mean you and your family? I think you may be getting ahead of yourself, but, yes, we can meet again tomorrow"

"Yes, I know my family may be in danger, and I want to strike preemptively before any harm comes to them. But there are many others who could be targets. Can we meet at two back here?"

"Let me check. Make it two-thirty. Okay?"

"Great, see you then."

ᴄᴈᴇᴈ

The list is three pages long.

"Commander, there are a total of sixty-two names, addresses, and telephone numbers of federal and city employees plus the two juries, who were involved in the case and the two trials. Chris and Brendan have noted those on the list that are deceased or have moved out of the area. The remaining list totals twenty-nine—twenty-nine individuals, who should be protected from the killers by the police department. Of the twenty-nine, fourteen should be considered most vulnerable to attacks from the murderers. These include foremen of the two juries, the prosecutors, Chris, Brendan, and me, as well as those who testified at the trials or spoke to the media."

"Okay, you've done your homework. This is an impressive list. What do you want me to do with this information?"

"Well, first and foremost, we should notify the federal attorney of our findings. Then the fourteen should be contacted, apprised of the situation, and given police protection. Some of that protection will come from the NYPD and some will be provided by the feds. As a civilian, this is almost as far as I can go, unless..."

"Unless what, Captain?"

"Unless I can reach out to the federal attorney as a private citizen acting at the behest of the NYPD."

"That's a big stretch. I don't think it's in the department's best interest to have a civilian do its bidding."

"All I need is a name and an introduction. I'll take from there and keep you in the loop. I ask for no credit. I only ask that I be able to serve the citizens of this city by putting a stop to the murders. I don't ask to be reinstated to the force. I just want to work with all interested parties to catch these killers."

Sometimes the promise of a noble cause is a viable way out for a bureaucrat.

"I need to discuss this with a few of the other commanders, before I green light your efforts."

"With all due respect, sir, I believe you have already discussed this with another commander or two. Any further discussion could take days, sir. And I'm concerned that we don't have days. Lives are in danger, and I would hate to have someone else die while you and I waited for a sanctioned approval. Plus, any extra hands could simply muck up the operation as others sought to direct it or take credit for it. Better to tell everyone what you have done than ask for permission to do something they would approve anyway."

"Interesting. I want it perfectly clear that you're operating under my guidance. Is that understood?"

"Yes."

"Do you have a few extra minutes now to draw up a contract between us? I'll have one of the administrative assistants work with you to draw it up. It will outline your facts and assumptions, as well as your desired course of action, and the requested guidance of the police department. You'll take full responsibility for your actions and report to me on a regular basis. As a civilian, you'll be operating way below the radar. We need to keep this between us as long as we can. You'll need to work with the admin in a conference room, and I'll review the document before we both sign it. Is this understood?"

"Yes, sir, and thank you."

The document preparation should take a little more than an hour. Officer Lamb is dutiful. She sits before her laptop and enters his words. Instantly, she has the first draft for review and minor fixes. The final document is ready for Vincent's review in an hour and a half. Tony wonders how much of his conversation with Officer Lamb is picked up by the bugs in the conference room.

"Looks good to me. I can sign this on behalf of the department. We must alert the various precincts about the need for them to provide protection to people on the list who live in their area. I'll take care of that because it requires someone above the precinct captain level to advise and alert the proper authorities. Once the document is signed, you're on your own. I'll help you insofar as my actions are positive, non-intrusive with the daily precinct operations and well below the One PP radar until we've reached a satisfactory conclusion. I want you to call Paul Tybor. He's in the federal attorney's office, and he can make things happen for you. By the way, what precautions are you taking for you, your family, and former team members?"

"Lieutenants McLaughlin and Wills have moved into hotels for the time being. I'll address these issues with my wife tonight. I can't thank you enough for your help in this matter."

"Jerry Aylir called and told me you needed someone to cut away the bureaucratic thistles. I'm always willing to listen to Jerry and help wherever I can. He has always been a big supporter of the force. Remember to let me know of your progress by next Friday. Here's my personal cell phone number. Use it."

Vincent wants to be able to take credit, but insists on credible deniability in case the bottom drops out and Tony screws up. Why did Vincent make it easy for Tony to get back in? What hold does Jerry Aylir have over Commander Vincent? *BINGO!* Eight years ago there was a huge and ever-growing budget crunch. So the city looked to the police, fire, and sanitation departments to cut back. The three departments decided it was less painful to reduce their operating budgets by forcing early retirement onto the fifteen to seventeen percent of their members who had been on the city dole for twenty years. This step would not deny a pension to those who were forced to retire, but the pensions received would just be smaller— fifty to sixty-five percent now versus the one-hundred percent they were promised in five years. The city commissioners were beseeched by many of those being forced out. Vincent was one of those. Jerry took up his case personally, based on their ties via Brooklyn Community College. Both men had risen and prospered nicely from the humble beginnings. Vincent owed Jerry the equivalent of $20,000 to $25,000 per year during retirement. Jerry paid it forward with PBA money. Very shrewd.

Twice during the subway trip uptown, Tony thought he was being followed. He thought he recognized the dark black skin and angular facial features of a man on the train. So he exited, went out to the street, and caught the next train on the line. No man. Paranoia is creeping in.

⁂

"What the hell are you saying? I'm under the threat of murder, my babies are in danger. What about my parents?"

"Melissa, please, honey, listen to me. First, your parents are in no danger, because they were not involved in the case. Second, we live in a penthouse that's very secure. There'll be regular visits from a patrol car to ensure your safety. I'll alert the building management to what's going on. They and I will alert the building staff to be on their toes. Third, the children are taken to and from school by Adolfo. I'll talk to him about varying his routes, and to be sure not to drive away until the children are in the school or our building. Fourth, wherever you go for the next few weeks, you must go with Adolfo. Is that understood? And fifth, since you have a concealed weapon permit, you must carry your gun whenever you leave the house. And six, we'll talk to Carmelita about her schedule and shopping habits. They must not be the same three days in a row. See, everything's covered. It won't take long for us to catch these perps. Okay?"

"Okay. What do we tell the children?"

"As little as possible. No need to scare the crap out of them. I'll—no, we'll—tell them now."

The children take all of the news and preparations in stride. Antonio wants to know if he could carry a gun. Bartheleme asks how this would affect his after school play practice. It is agreed that Adolfo would arrive at school in time to pick up the children after baseball and play practice. During this extra time at school, Cassandra could finish her homework. But she must stay in the school building. Melissa would notify the school of their plan. Cassandra suggested they each carry a Bobby whistle—that shrill alarm item carried by London's finest. He will buy four tomorrow. Melissa wants one.

Sleep is not easy. Too many convoluted images. Too much violence. It's time to get down to the heart of the matter. Should Tony get Adolfo a gun in violation of his parole?

Chapter 6

On the way downtown to the federal building, To-ny feels the eyes of another dark black, angular-faced stranger. He decides not to change trains, but anxiety builds. He sweats and his pulse rate is way too high. He changes cars and the man is no longer visible. Is Tony next?

Paul Tybor is a tall, well-groomed man with a ready smile. His corner office is big, but not huge. It is cluttered with stacks of files and reports. There are twelve stacks on the table and four on Paul's desk. There are even stacks in the office corners. In this electronic age, paper stacks make Tony feel comfortable. He feels he can trust this man.

"Captain, how can I help you?"

"Sir—"

"Call me Paul, please."

"Paul, I believe we have a situation brewing that will impact both of us and therefore we need to work together to resolve it. Let me lay it out for you."

Tony proceeds to walk Paul through the facts and as-sumptions. Most important is the list of the federal employees and witnesses involved with the trial—those who could be in grave danger.

"Assuming all of this is accurate, I can get to these people to alert them of the possible danger, and I'll call the US Marshall Service to arrange for soft protection—surveillance of home, trips and work place. I assumed from my conversation with Commander Vincent, that he is taking the same appropriate steps."

How much did Vincent tell him? Is Tony the messenger or the fall guy? Certainly, he'll not be the hero.

"Paul, I will now ask a big favor of you and your office? I would like to review all of the activity of Ms. Razdarovich, Ms. Linder, and Makeda. I would like to see visitor logs, telephone conversations, and written correspondence for the three women who were are the core of the illegal enterprise. This information may give us some clues as to what they may be plotting."

"Well, Ms. Razdarovich and Ms. Linder died in prison. The Russian was shanked about two years ago, and Ms. Linder suffered a massive heart attack and died in the prison hospital four years ago. There was conjecture that she was poisoned with an exotic drug that causes the heart to literally deteriorate in two days. A small scratch was found in her neck, but the prison coroner was not equipped to do extensive testing, was understaffed, and deemed the mark innocuous and thus ruled out murder. He listed simple heart attack as the COD. No autopsy was performed."

"Who shanked Ms. Razdarovich?"

"A biker bitch serving twenty years for Murder Two—the killing of three women at a bar. She's now serving her complete sentence plus fifteen years. It was a federal case because the biker gang was under our surveillance for interstate trafficking in meth and heroin. The three women were just patrons at the bar, but were thought to be CIs for us. They were not our CIs. The biker bitch was the old lady of the leader of a gang known as Archangels. A very tough crew here in the Northeast that distributes through schools from Maine to Virginia. They fear no one. Not us. Not local cops. Not other gangs. They make the Mongols look like crybabies."

"Did Ms. Linder have any enemies in prison?"

"Oddly enough, she seemed able to avoid confrontation. She never had many friends, but she had no enemies. Another reason the death was not ruled suspicious."

"I know these three fell under your jurisdiction so they went to federal prisons in various locations. So, after I review all the prison records, I'd like to talk to Makeda, if that would be possible."

"Jesus, her new name is Katherine Elizabeth Samuels, and she's in the women's ultra max prison in Wayfar, Colorado. She gets one hour each day out of her cell for exercise, her telephone privileges are limited to one call out each month and one call in each week. Her written correspondence is read, copied, and sent if deemed nonthreatening. She is in real lock down."

"Sir, I believe that the three murders outlined in my document are connected to the men who were soldiers at the mission and who are now out on parole. These men were sheep in Makeda's flock then, and it would not surprise me that they're sheep in Ms. Samuel's flock now. I need to know if she's involved. If she's not, we have a small but aggressive universe of bad guys. If she *is* calling the shots, we've stumbled upon a far-reaching, very-dangerous, well-organized gang of killers. I need your help to answer these questions. But, to get to the bottom of all this, I need to talk to the former Makeda. Is that possible?"

"You're asking a lot. But if I send you as my personal assistant, I think you could clear the screening process and see Ms. Samuels. I can pull all the records you want. Then we'll talk about how to get you the Wayfar."

"Thank you, Paul. When should I come back here to look at the prison files?"

"Give me a week."

Jerry pulls Vincent's chain so he helps Tony. Then to show how far Vincent will go to thank Jerry, Vincent prods Paul Tybor to help. The inner workings of the good-old-boy network throughout various city and federal agencies are mind boggling.

❧❧❧

Tony goes to the Day School in search of the science lab. Second floor East. He peers through the window in the door and sees about a dozen children tinkering, pouring, watching and noting results in notebooks. No Cassandra. He enters. There she is standing in front of a huge white board. She is surveying boxes containing words, the lines connecting the boxes, and the words on the lines. Tony is immediately confronted by the science teacher, a very attractive woman in her mid-thirties.

"May I help you?"

"Yes, I'm Tony Sattill, Cassandra's father. I just dropped by to see how she was coming on her science project."

"Daddy, no! You can't see it yet. It's not ready."

"Well, I guess you have your answer."

"Okay. I'll obey her wishes. But before I leave with my tail between my legs, will you explain what she's doing at the white board, while all the other children are performing real lab experiments?"

"Let's step outside. I don't use this term lightly, but your daughter's gifted. Are you aware of the string theory?"

"Vaguely."

"Well, Cassandra has morphed the string theory and simplified it to an understandable Theory of Connectivity. This is the theory that everything we know, or do, is based on math and therefore connected."

"That's too far afield for me."

"Let me give you an example. Math is the basis for all thought because it's basis for logic. Math and logic are directly connected to science. Science is connected to agriculture, the arts, war, and transportation, etc. Your daughter's demonstrating these connections. She's writing the connections, examples and how these are connected to other facets of our life. She's very, very smart. The Day School is just beginning to recognize exceptional students like Cassandra. We need the cooperation of parents to ensure this type of talent isn't squandered."

"Excuse me, but damn! Cassandra's mother and I never knew."

"She wants to surprise her family. So let her."

"Yes, ma'am."

❧❧❧

"Adolfo, I need to talk with you about an important and very private matter."

"Sure thing, Mr. Sattill. I'll meet you in the garage."

The basement of the condo building has parking slots for thirty cars. There are forty units in the building. Some of the residents feel cheated. The lucky ones pay an extra $1,000 per month for the privilege of keeping their $100,000 autos close at hand. Adolfo lives twelve blocks from the condo. So he's available nearly immediately when needed.

"What's all the mystery about, Mr. Sattill?"

Tony explains what has happened, what might happen, and what Adolfo can do to prevent any problems from befalling Tony's family.

"I'm going to give you a piece. I know you're not allowed to carry a weapon because of your legal situation. And I know the weapon's unregistered. But I know you know how to use a hand gun and would only do so judiciously. Given the circumstances, Mrs. Sattill and I would feel better if you carried this gun when you drive the children to school and when you take Mrs. Sattill on her day trips. I also want you to vary your routes to and from the school, and take circuitous routes for Mrs. Sattill's day trips. I need you to do this until we get some answers. Is all this clear?"

"Yes, sir, it's clear. If I get nabbed with the piece, do I call you?"

"Yes, but before that I'll let our local precinct captain, Captain Evers, know what I've done, and why. One more thing, this gun has serial numbers and is on file with the NYPD. It has my name attached to it. It was key to a case I closed twenty years ago. The property master needed a favor."

Adolfo takes the .380 and places in his pants waist directly over his butt crack. Tony hands him a second clip. He now has sixteen hollow-point high-load bad guy killers. One hit and the bad guy stays down.

"I guarantee that nothing will happen to your wife or children. I owe you my life, so I'll protect them with mine."

They shake hands and each departs the way he entered the garage.

෧෨෫

"Captain, I have some preliminary information about

Ellis and Abraham. Until about five years ago, both of their communication with the outside world was limited to their lawyers on average once every three months. Then, five years ago, which is two years before they could expect their earliest release both men were in contact with a new lawyer each month. This new lawyer's name is Eliot Livingston. I checked this guy out and he is the same suit who represented the three women at arraignment and Makeda at trial. Over the last two years of their incarceration, they each received visits from Mr. Livingston every three months under the guise of helping them get ready for freedom. I have to do more digging on this angle, but I find it very interesting, don't you?"

"It could be a coincidence."

"Captain, you trained me that there are no coincidences in crime, just unknown facts."

"Good catch, Brendan. Anything else?"

"According to prison documents and the Head of the Guards I spoke to, Ellis and Abraham were on speaking terms with a prison gang known for drug distribution on the East Coast. The gang is named the Archangels. I never heard of them, but that's not my area of expertise. So I reached out to a buddy in Narcotics, and he told me the Archangels are one of if not the most vicious gang of drug dealers on the radar. Yearly narco raids yield pounds of meth and heroin. But their coffers seem to be refilled within three months. The gang seems to have a mobile headquarters. The narcs, state and federal, never hit the same place twice. My buddy, indicated, that the word on the street is that there will be a big sale within the next two months.

The gang's name registers with Tony. A series of connections is beginning to emerge.

"Great job, Brendan. How's hotel life?"

"Well, I leave and return at different times and move on different routes each day. I spend weekends out of the city. Nice meals and a good gym. It's getting expensive."

"Keep a diary and all receipts. You'll get reimbursed each month. Stay with it, buddy. Let's talk next week. Thanks for all your work. Chris, what about you? What did you learn?"

"Damn. Brendan stole my story. Everything, but the names. The timing, the visits, the communications, and the Archangels are the same for Benny Radle and Ernest Davis. I spoke to a friend of mine in the Gang Unit. She told me where the Archangels have their present head-quarters—if that matters."

"Matters? Hell, yes. That's key to gaining more knowledge."

"Now the question is how do we speak to the Arch-angels without being nailed as cops, and without screw-ing up any investigation by Narcotics and the Gang Unit?"

"Good question. I have no answer. Brendan, what about you?"

"Captain, I got nothing. Let me sleep on it and I'll call both of you tomorrow at ten a.m. Okay?"

"Okay, and, guys, Jamie would be proud of you. Remember how she watched your work like a mother hen. And she would be honored that you're doing this for her. We'll talk tomorrow.

⁊

"Tony, what in God's name do you mean? What the hell are you doing?"

"I'll explain, Melissa. Chris, Brendan, and I believe we've discovered a link between the murders of Jamie, Joan Mussleman, and Thomas Clarkton. A link that could lead to a very large conspiracy, and we need to follow the evidence to confirm our suspicions."

"I know the three of you. You'll be just on the fringe of legality. Actually, you'll be operating outside the law."

"We're just concerned citizens."

"Bullshit. I know you have permission from the police force to pursue this matter. Your involvement started with you just observing. Now, it has ballooned into a full-fledged investigation and you have no authority. I can only assume that you have contacted the federal prosecutor and secured his nod of approval to proceed. Both the NYPD and the feds have allowed you—no, encouraged you—to walk to the end of the limb in reach for the most precious fruit. If you fall off the limb and break your neck before you get the fruit, it'll be your fault. If you get the fruit and hand it over to the legal authorities, they'll take all the credit for the investigation, and you'll be referred in the footnotes as an anonymous contributor.

"All the while your ass is on the line. All risk and no reward. Great fucking concept. Your future actions will, no doubt, put you and your family in greater danger than exists already. But, hell, big bad Tony doesn't see it that way. He sees himself as the knight in shining armor riding to save the day. It's the same situation as that damned Mission investigation fifteen years ago, except the really bad people are in jail, you're fifteen years older, and you have a wife and three children who could be killed."

"I see my work as helping to solve three murders. Most importantly, solve the murder of Jamie Lanno, who was part of my family before I had a family. She would do the same for me, just as I would do the same if one of my family today were murdered or severely injured. And how did you learn about my contact with the force?"

"Then it's revenge. The Russians have a saying that revenge is like borscht, a dish best served cold. I learned that from the evil Mrs. Razdarovich. My source? He's my father, and I'm his only child—a daughter. Tony, I'm frightened for you, for my babies, and for me. The more you try to resolve or solve this situation, the more danger we're in and the more pressure there is on you to protect us."

"As for protection, I've taken all the necessary steps. And, tonight will either confirm or deny the existence of a true conspiracy. So we're nearly out of the woods. I'll turn over all my findings to the force and the federal prosecutor and wait for their decision. Now I have to get some sleep. I'm being picked-up by Brendan and Chris at two. I'll be home before breakfast. You'll never know I'm gone."

"Bull."

⁊⁊⁊

"Help! Help! Help! Somebody, come quick. This man needs help."

"What seems to be the problem?"

"Officer, look. He's bleeding"

There was William Swarts, sitting face up on the platform of the IRT Number Four line. Blood was oozing from his neck and eye sockets. His eyes had been re-moved. The transit patrolman called in the mess. Within ten minutes, the area was a yellow-taped island. The can-vass revealed nothing. Mr. Swarts still wore his watch and wedding band. There was eighty-six dollars in his wallet. Not a robbery. Just a very ugly murder.

New York Ledger Wednesday, April 4, 2014
Business Man Killed in Subway
Mr. William Swarts, Executive Vice President of AMC Communications, was found murdered at the 77th

Street station of the IRT line at approximately 10:30 p.m. on Tuesday. The police are asking anyone who may have knowledge of the murder to please contact their local precinct. Mr. Swarts, a resident of Manhattan's upper East Side, leaves behind a life partner.

Chapter 7

"Hi, guys."

"Hi, Captain."

"We're good to go. And where are we going, Chris?"

"A side street off the Brooklyn-Queens Expressway. About One Hundred Thirty-Fifth Avenue in Jackson Heights. Looks more like an alley. One way in and the same way out. My guess is that are no street lights, a ton of trash, iron gates, and nasty dogs. Other than that, just a pleasant stroll in the park."

"Where did you get this rust bucket?"

"Impound. It has been left outside in the elements for a few years. And it's a regular vehicle for stakeouts. Very indistinguishable from other neighborhood wrecks, except for the engine and tires. Four hundred and fifty horses push huge BMW racing tires. A muscle man in the disguise of an octogenarian."

"Very nice, Brendan."

The trip takes thirty minutes of winding streets to avoid ant detection. No sense in tipping our hand. There it is the dark alley, just like Chris described it. Leaving the car at the mouth of the alley, the three men dressed in black with black ski masks open the creaking doors and proceed the seventy-five feet to the chained gate. When they arrive at the iron door, they hear the deep throated growls of what must be very big and very nasty dogs. At least two. Maybe three. There are no lights on in the building behind the gate and none come on with the growls. The place is empty or the denizens are passed out. Tony hopes for the former.

"Before we breach, let's be sure what we're going to do."

"Chris, do you have the darts and dart gun for the dogs? I assume you can reload the damned thing after the first sleep tonic is delivered to the dog or dogs. You may need a dart or two for anyone in the club house."

"Yes and yes. I have seven darts, just in case."

"Brendan, you have the bolt cutters and taser?"

"Yes, and I have a taser for each of us for use with on live-in baddies."

"My guess is that the place is also wired to a silent alarm system that rings at the president's home. We'll have about twelve minutes to get in and out safely. Watch your step."

"Captain, we're ready."

"Sorry, I'm nearly as rusty as the car. Just doing my due diligence."

The chain links are about one-half an inch thick. Brendan has to use a double cut to make one complete through and through. Then a second set of cuts to break the link in half. The growls are now louder and closer. The two dogs are standing guard just behind the gate. Chris inserts the darts in gun. Schwup! A whine and one hound is down. Schwup! The second dog is down.

"Guys, we have ten minutes of non-intervention. If we need much longer, I'll give the dogs another tap."

"Fifteen minutes out cold will have to do. Brendan, check the front door for an alarm."

"All clear. Going in slowly. Guys, there are two snoring bodies on couches, what should I do?"

"Wait for Chris. He'll keep them in the land of nod with his darts."

Schwup! Schwup!

"Now it's safe to rummage around."

"What are we looking for?"

"Any kind of clue that connects the Archangels to Benny Radle, David Ellis, Wilson Abraham, and Ernest Davis. Chris, check the back room. It looks like an office."

"Captain, look at these crates. I'll need to use the bolt cutter. The crates are secured with big padlocks. Whoa—do automatic weapons count as good evidence?"

"No, but we'll take them all so this intrusion will look like a robbery…maybe by a rival gang."

"There must be twenty-five autos here—Mac Tens, AKs, Glocks. No Desert Eagle Fifty. And many boxes of ammo."

"We'll each carry some when we leave. Brendan, bring me the cutters. The closet is locked tight."

"Captain, I found a notebook with a lot of initials and dates in it. If I could understand the code, I'd say it was the mother lode."

"Grab it. Anything else?"

"Money. A big wooden box of money. Hundreds stacked and in nice neat bundles. If I had to guess, I couldn't. The box is too big."

"Time's up. Let us exit forthwith."

Brendan and Tony grab the weapons for departure, while Chris leaves with the notebook and big box of money. They quietly close the gate and walk quickly to the car. All items are placed in the trunk, they enter, and

Brendan guns the engine beating a hasty retreat. As they turn the corner, they notice two cars rushing into the alley. Close but no cigar. Now back to Brandon's precinct to log in the evidence. While Brendan follows protocol, Chris goes home and Tony secretly copies each page of the notebook before it becomes legal evidence. He needs to examine it in detail.

∽◦∽

Slipping between the sheets, Tony has ninety minutes before he must become a husband and father.

"Be quiet, my husband might hear you. He's a very possessive Italian. Oh, Tony, it's you."

"Is that you, Jennifer? Oh, my God, where am I? Is that you, Melissa?"

They giggle and snuggle.

∽◦∽

Breakfast is consumed amidst the clamor of three hyper teens. Adolfo arrives in time to save Tony from screaming. Melissa wants to go downtown to the spa, then shopping, then lunch with a few old friends, who are on most of the same charitable committees. She knows to carry her gun. She will call at each stop. This process makes him feel safe. Adolfo attention to Tony's family makes Tony feel safe. To the solarium and the notebook pages.

"Captain, did you see who was murdered last night, while we were working?"

"Haven't looked at the news, Chris."

"Mr. William Swarts. He was a major witness at both the state and federal trials of the three women. He was a CPA who reviewed the mission books and the bank books. He had copious meeting notes that laid out the criminal enterprise."

"Oh, now I recall."

"And the gory part is that his eyes were cut out of his sockets. My friend at the ME's office told me the excising was done before his throat was slit. There had to be more than one murderer. My guess is there were three—two to hold him down and one to slice and dice. These guys are really sending messages loud and clear."

"I'll put a bug in the ears of the department and the federal prosecutor. They better circle the wagons today and protect all those that remain. Have you looked to see if you're being followed?"

"I take a different path home and to the precinct each day. I stop along the way for coffee or a beer going home to watch who is behind me. So far nada. How about you?"

"I thought I saw someone the other week, but I must have imagined it. I'll check with Brendan. Don't do anything more until I contact you. Thanks, Chris. You've done yeoman's work."

"I had a good teacher. Talk soon."

෴

"One million dollars and enough weapons and ammo for a militia-size army," Brendan says. "That's some serious shit, Captain. I had to tell my captain how I got all of this evidence. It was an anonymous tip from the federal prosecutor. I forgot to include you and Chris in my report. You both have culpable deniability. I asked two of my CAT team members if they would stand in for you two. So the raid was conducted by me and Officers Brent and Jamison. You better call the federal guy and fill him immediately, because I know my captain will contact him today. The police cannot arrest the Archangels on weapons charges, because no police were at the club house to seize the weapons, because there was no probable cause and, therefore, no warrant. Thomason better keep an eye on these bastards. There may be repercussions. I'll call Chris and tell him."

"Jesus, Brendan, it's beginning to make some sense. Your pal in narcotics said the Archangels were about to make a huge buy. The cash is certainly enough to make a huge buy. The gang then turns around and sells the stuff to dealers at five to seven times their purchase price. Now you're looking at five plus million dollars. With that kind of money they can buy a ton of allegiance with the street thugs and arm some of them as body guards. They're building a real army. This smells vaguely reminiscent of the Mission army. Do I see the relationship, or is it just wishful thinking?"

"I think we're on to something very big and very bad. Maybe the notebook will tells us more. The brain trust at the precinct is looking over the pages. This case has taken on a life of its own. Hell, my captain even called Thomason to bring him into the loop. I'm sure Thomason called his rabbi at One PP to complain about being excluded. But those are the breaks. If I had the notebook pages, I would go over them with a very discerning eye. But I don't have the book or even copies of the pages."

"Thanks for the heads up. I'll call the federal prosecutor. We must now lay low. How long? I don't know, but I'll let you know when we can resume our activities. I can't thank you enough. Jamie sends her best—and that was damned good."

The forty single-sided Xerox pages sit in a stack on Tony's left. He needs a nap.

His power nap lasts two hours. Age and yesterday's late hour will do that. He calls Tybor, tells him what he should know, and reminds him he wants to see Makeda or Samuels. Tybor promises to call back today or tomorrow. Then he calls Vincent and tells him a little less. Keep them both in the loop, just not letting them control the work. Tony splashes his face with cold water, pours a cup of fresh coffee, and begins his homework.

He strokes over repeated items with different colored highlighter pens. After a quick read through, a pattern begins to emerge. He sees sets of initials appearing frequently on the pages. BR/DE/WA/ED must stand for Benny Radle, David Ellis, Wilson Abraham, and Ernst Davis, the four Ethiopians who were in The Mission's army. Also every so often the initials KES and EL appeared on the same pages that preceded the pages that contained the four sets of initials. Time sequence. Did the Archangels get some form of communication or information from KES and EL and then pass it along to the four foot soldiers? There are no telephone numbers only a group of words and near words on the front page of the book. Words like NOLEADS and WASHINGTON. What kind of code is that?

Did the four soldiers act at the command of KES and EL? KES always appears before EL. Who are KES and EL? Bingo! EL is Eliot Livingston. He is the lawyer for Makeda and the four bad guys. Okay. Then who is KES? There are dates and corresponding numbers like twenty-five or forty-seven or sixty-two. Are these collection dates and amounts collected? Then a strange entry manifests itself—EL appears before KES. Out of sequence or were the Archangels reporting back through Eliot Livingston to KES? Then the initials JL next to a date, TC a week later, and JM about a week after that. The victims and the murder dates. Were all the murders committed by the four bad guys, and did the Archangels keep score? So they could report back to Eliot and KES? The Archangels played a large part in the plan. Who killed Swarts?

There is one date, April twenty-eighth, with no notation. But the entry was traced over and over again. It must be important. The delivery of the drugs. Tony must let Brendan, Vincent, and Tybor know what he has found.

⌘

New York Ledger Wednesday, April 11, 2014
NYPD Lieutenant Dead at Home
Lieutenant Willard "Tommy" Thomason was found dead in his home in Jackson Heights, Queens on Tuesday. Lieutenant Thomason had a long and illustrious career with the New York City Police Department. He died of an apparent accidental gun discharge. He is survived by his wife, Dorothy, and two adult children who live in California. There will be a memorial mass at Our Lady of Abiding Love. 1445 Queens Boulevard on Friday, April 13 2013 at 2 p.m.

"Who knows what?"

"Captain—"

"Okay, guys, please call me Tony. I'm not your, or anyone's, captain. I'm retired, remember."

"Okay."

"Okay."

"Well the death is suspicious. According to the ME, Thomason could not have shot himself from five feet away. Second, his side arm was a departmental-issued forty-five, and he was shot with a fifty-caliber Desert Eagle. Third, he was shot three times. What are the odds the murder was committed by the Archangels as payback for the robbery of their club house? If that's true, then it's safe to say that Thomason was deep into the Archangels. Pay to play. They apparently thought that they were not getting their money's worth. So they did away with the offender."

"Chris, I think you're spot on."

"I'll bet the force raids the club house today or tomorrow, looking for the Desert Eagle, and discovers the weapons and cache of cash."

"Brendan, what do you mean? Our beloved force doing something unethical and illegal. Why that's unheard of. I'm shocked."

"It would be easy to drop an assault rifle or two in each room and discover the box-o-booty by sheer happenstance. All during the normal search. The force would get the credit for our work."

"That would take us off the hook. Shall we make book on when the raid, discovery, and arrests are announced."

"I'll take by five today."

"Okay, Brendan."

"I'll take noon tomorrow."

"Okay, Chris. That leaves me with five tomorrow."

"Is fifty bucks all right with you guys?"

"Yep."

"Yep."

∽∾∽

"This is News Breaker Nine, Your Source for All That Matters.

"We go live to the borough of Queens where the New York City Police Department has conducted a raid on the club house of the notorious Motorcycle Club, the Archangels. Our reporter at the scene is Stephanie Snyder. Stephanie, what can you tell us?"

"At two-thirty today, about thirty minutes ago, the NYPD raided the club house of the Archangels gang, notorious for alleged drug and weapons distribution. The police were acting on an anonymous tip and discovered numerous automatic weapons, a grenade launcher, boxes of ammunition, and a substantial amount of cash. In addition numerous members of the gang were arrested. A spokesman for the police department stated that this takes an extensive amount of danger off the streets, and makes Queens and all of New York much safer. As you can see behind me, there are the weapons, ammunition, and the box that allegedly contains about three-quarters of a million dollars. We'll try to get statements from the arresting officers, and report as more unfolds. For now, this is Stephanie Snyder."

ᗢᗢᗢ

Tony hopes that any difference in the cash discovered during his raid and the department's raid will find its way into the widows' and orphans' fund. He wonders if they found the basis for their search—the .50 Desert Eagle. It would be easy to "drop" the any Desert Eagle and claim they found it along with the weapons, ammo, and money which were all in plain sight. If not, the force will be in deep caca. In a rush to judgment, the predictable police force may have shot itself in its collective feet. Tony's father was right—the advantage of telling the truth is that you don't have to remember what lie you told. His nap was interrupted by the blathering talking heads. Back to the nap.

ᗢᗢᗢ

"Next case."

"Docket Number five-three-four-nine-zero-zero-six, the People versus members of the motorcycle club, the Archangels. The defendants are…"

"For the defense?"

"Eliot Livingston, your honor."

"How do the defendants plead?"

"Not guilty. The police conducted an illegal and warrantless search of a private club."

"The people request that each of the defendants be remanded without bail. These are hardened criminals who pose a threat to society and a substantial flight risk."

"My clients are going nowhere, because this case is based on an illegal search. They wish to have the case dismissed based on a paucity of true evidence."

"That will be up to the trial judge, Mr. Livingston. For now, each will be responsible for two hundred thousand dollars cash or bond."

As the assistant DA is walking out of the courtroom, he's approached by a man, very small in stature, perhaps five feet or five feet two inches in height. His black hair is slicked back and forms little ringlets at the back if his shirt collar. He's clean shaven. His suit is obviously tailored made to his shape and weight, and his foulard complements his monochromatic red tie. His shirt is light blue with a white collar and cuffs. His Italian shoes are appropriately pointed and very shiny. On his right hand pinky finger is a large gold ring, and his watch is a Gold Rolex. His eyes are constantly darting left and right, and his teeth are capped brilliant white. He wears the latest cologne from Europe. A little too much. In another environment, he would be called a dandy or a Banty, short for a Bantam Roster.

"Mr. Breathson, can we talk?"

"About what, Mr. Livingston?"

"About my motion, the illegal search, the items found, and the item not found."

"Explain yourself."

"The warrant that was the basis for the illegal search was never executed properly. Instead, the city Gestapo crashed into the private club house of my clients and conveniently found items that the police felt would make a good case against my clients. If you have fifteen minutes in your office, I'll explain all the details."

"Let' talk here and now."

"That would be fine with me. As you can see, the warrant clearly specifies the search was conducted to secure a Desert Eagle Fifty hand gun. Now, if you examine the inventory of items confiscated, there is no such gun listed, because it was not there. A second aspect of the search and seizure is the confiscation of numerous automatic weapons and ammunition that was in plain sight. I have downloaded the crime scene video that was aired on television. You'll note there are padlocks on the floor next to the two crates in the main room and one padlock next to the closet in the office. All three locks were cut with a bolt cutter before the crates and closet were opened. Thus, the contents of the three areas were not in plain sight. Thus, the police had no legal cause to secure the items. The third factor is that the box of money found in the closet contained one million dollars not seven hundred and fifty thousand dollars. My clients have records to show how much money was in the box and the dates it was acquired. So, you can see clearly that, if you proceed down this path, you'll be laughed out of court and subject to a civil suit of at least eleven million dollars—one million for each defendant."

"You allegations are interesting. My office will take it under advisement."

"If I don't hear from you by two this afternoon, I'll hold a press conference outlining the flaws in the case. The court of public opinion will free my clients and run you out of town on a rail."

Case dismissed. The "extra" money is still missing. The Archangels consider the lost cash to be tribute unto Caesar. They can replace that amount in about six weeks. The planned transaction may have to be delayed.

Chapter 8

aptain Sattill, this is Paul Tybor. We have clearance for you to spend a few hours with Katherine Elizabeth Samuels. The visit is all set for the day after tomorrow. No time has been set. After you make your plane reservations to Denver, let me know the details, and I'll forward them to my contact at the federal penitentiary. He will arrange to pick you up, get you to the penitentiary, and get you back to Denver in time to fly home. The trip to and from the airport takes about an hour and one-half. If you need to stay overnight, I very strongly suggest it be at the Denver airport—not at the facility."

"Thanks, Paul, I appreciate the help. I'll call you in a few hours with my itinerary."

Katherine Elizabeth Samuels is still pulling the strings even from an ultra-max federal facility in Wayfar, Colorado. What is her game plan? American Express books the flights to and from so that the only over-night is after the interview. Tony will fly out early in the morning, interview in the afternoon, and fly back to his family the next morning. After he tells Tybor, he must tell Melissa.

"You're like a fraternity boy drinking blue blazers. You remember, you light the brandy in a shot glass. The match ignites a blue flame. Then you throw the flaming liquid into your mouth and swallow it before the blue flame becomes a hot issue. If you miss even slightly, you'll burn your lips, maybe your face, and maybe even your hair. Risk and reward for the testosterone starved assholes of our era. Braggadocio and bravado lived after hours in the basement bars.

"You think there is a connection between the Mission family and the recent murders, so you want to go to the person you think is at the core of the crimes. But she's locked down in a federal penitentiary in Bumfuck, Colorado. If you piss her off, she may send her minions after you, me, and our babies. If she has enough power to lure you out to the hell hole from nowhere, she may have enough power to get us all. Did you ever think of that, Sir Knight Errant? Yes, I'm scared, because you're putting us in jeopardy. Maybe, until this bullshit is resolved, I should take the children out of school and move to Canada...some chalet in the mountains. We can wait for you to slay the dragon and then rescue us from the Canadians.

"Melissa, I know you're frightened. And, to some degree, I can't blame you. But you have to understand that I'm the only guy who can resolve all of this. The feds won't touch it, and the NYPD just had its case against the Archangels tossed. I'm it."

"You're it, because you want to be it. You like the concept of the noble lone hero fighting against all odds to make the world safe."

"Is that bad or wrong?"

"It's only wrong when your actions put those you love in jeopardy. It's called being reckless. And I have a real problem with you being reckless with the lives of my children."

"Look, I'll fly out early tomorrow morning and be back before dinner the next day. I'll take cabs, and ask Adolfo to stay with you guys for the two half days and one night. Cassandra can sleep with you, and Adolfo can sleep in her room. You have a gun. He has a gun. The elevators doors can be locked. You'll be safe, I promise."

"You're a rotten shit, Tony, when you explain everything so that I can't worry."

"I plan things so you'll be safe, because I love you more than life itself."

"And, by the by, who are the Archangels?"

"A motor cycle gang tied to everyone in this cabal. Hell, they may even be the driving force."

"Oh, great, now I have to watch out for leather clad bullies on noisy bikes. Will this crap ever end?"

"Soon, very soon, I promise."

ၽ

Southwest Airlines flight 544 leaves LaGuardia at five forty-four a.m. and arrives on time in Denver at six forty-two a.m. local time. As Tony exits the terminal with his carry-on bag, he sees a state trooper holding piece of cardboard with the name *SATTILL*.

"That's me, Tony Sattill."

"May I see a picture ID?"

"Yes, my New York Driver's License. And you are?"

"Officer Jones, Robert Jones."

"May I see your ID, Officer Jones?"

Both identities confirmed, the men head out to the department of correction's Land Rover, properly unmarked. The tires are larger than normal, indicating lots of horse power and the mechanics to control them. Thirty minutes of silence is broken by Jones.

"New York, eh. You're a long way from home. Don't you have enough criminals in the big apple that you have to go to Colorado and speak to ours?"

"Actually, this prisoner is not yours. She belongs to the federal government. I'm here at the request of the federal prosecutor. Just doing what I'm told."

"Who's Katherine Elizabeth Samuels to you?"

"An acquaintance. Someone I met fifteen years ago, when she called herself Makeda. The federal prosecutor needs her help. Hopefully, I can learn something during my visit. What kind of inmate is she?"

"No big deal. She is kept in lock down twenty-two hours a day. She can exercise, go to the library, and shower during the other two hours. She sends letters. We read them and let them through. She gets letters. We read them and let them through. She makes a telephone call each month to her attorney. It would be against the law to listen or record those telephone calls. So we don't do either. Wink. Wink. She never gets visitors. You're the first in that category. We have thirty women of the same ilk. They're never getting out, so they live their lives the way they would in any new home."

The officer's speech pattern is slow and deliberate. He sounds as if he is bored. As the Land Rover comes to the crest of a small mountain…or large hill, Tony sees spread out before him a desolate valley. No trees or growth, just rocks and dirt. Very flat. In the center of and toward the end of the valley are several concrete structures. They are surrounded by two sets of fences and acres of nothing. There are towers at each corner of the compound. There is a single black top road leading into and out of the fenced in city.

"We'll be there in about thirty minutes. I'll take you to see the warden. He'll be your guide and contact while you're in the facility."

"Thanks."

"Nice to meet you. We don't get many people out here except those who will be staying for life. When you're ready to leave for the Denver airport, I'll drive you. Here's the first check point. Get your ID out."

One check point on the road and a second immediately before the prison, three gates, and an electric scanner protect the guards and criminals from outside evil influences.

"Warden Jenkins, this is Tony Sattill, or should I say Captain Antonio Sattill, New York City Police Department, retired."

"You're excused, Officer Jones. And thank you."

"Yes, thank you, Officer. Tony will do. Warden Jenkins, I appreciate your indulgence by letting me talk to Makeda—er—I mean Katherine Elizabeth Samuels. I'm sure federal attorney Paul Tybor filled you in on the objective of my visit."

"Not, really, why don't you tell me?"

Tony lays out all that he wants this stranger to know. If he told the warden everything, that might be a problem.

"Tony, I have collected all the information about Ms. Samuels's activities during her incarceration here at Wayfar. You may use my conference as your reading library. If you need anything copied, feel free to use the machine in the conference room. I'll let you alone. Your interview with Ms. Samuels is scheduled for one p.m. Right after her lunch. You and I will eat in the conference room. This will give me time to answer any questions you might have. That said, I will leave you alone. Oh, if you need to use the head, there's one off the conference room. Good luck."

Stacks of files contain reams of paper. When Tony opens the file folder marked Correspondence In, he notes hand written foot notes and references to pages in other files. All in all, the files are a plethora of near-meaningless minutia. During her first ten years at Way-far, her files reflect nothing spectacular. Not much correspondence. Two phone calls per year. Four years ago the flow of communications picked-up dramatically.

Monthly letters and telephone calls to and from Eliot Livingston, her recently chosen lawyer. The letters appear to be absent of any code, unless the weather, and times of sunrises and sunsets are coded messages. They may be the longings of a lonely human indulging in the smallest events. *Or* they could be a code. Tony makes copies of these pages, and the referenced pages in other files. He needs to get a weather report plus times of the sun activity for the days before the dates of the letters. He needs to hear the telephone calls between KES and EL. He will ask for copies of the telephone messages that precede the recent murders in New York.

After three hours of reading, he needs coffee. There is an empty pot in the coffee maker in the room. With the help of good detective work, he finds the paper filter and the coffee packets. In fifteen minutes, the black energizer is working. Now to the restroom. Some fluid in and some fluid out. Back to the files. Medical. Who cares? Dietary changes when she changed her name and religion. Now she can eat anything. There are no religious dietary restrictions on her life. Books she has read from the library. Modern romance. Her acquaintances and associates. None. She is a loner as befits a queen.

"Knock. Knock. Lunch time."

"My gawd, it's eleven thirty. I was having so much fun, that I lost track of time. I welcome the break, Warden. What's for lunch?"

"Fried chicken, potato salad, cole slaw, sour dough bread, and coffee. We have our food delivered weekly and cooked by the kitchen staff before they cook the meal for the inmates. We watch them very closely to be sure there's no spit, pins, urine, bugs, or rat droppings in our meals. Help yourself. I see you found the coffee. Now what questions do you have?"

"I need the transcripts of the telephone calls between Ms. Samuels and her lawyer, Eliot Livingston, for the past year. Not sure what if anything I'll find. But I think there may be some interesting dialogue. As to questions, I'm not yet well-versed in the subject of Ms. Samuels to ask reasonable questions. I'll say this, your information gathering and filing systems with the cross reference is damned good. It eased my knowledge intake of the woman in question."

"Let me be personal, Tony. What's your real interest in Ms. Samuels?"

"Ms. Samuels was named Makeda when I first met her. She and two other women ran a very evil international cartel hidden behind her outreach mission that was supposedly helping the downtrodden of New York City, but was exploiting the residents. The net of her life is that she's evil to her very core. And, I believe, she had a hand in the murder of one of my former team members, along with several people who were involved in her trial and conviction. I believe she's a big-time shot caller, as they're known in prison, but a shot caller to people on the outside. Thus, I need to talk to her."

"Then let's go meet her. Once you're situated in the interview room, we'll bring her to you. I'll get you transcripts of the telephone calls you noted. They'll be ready when you leave. I don't want to put any constraints on your time here, but we lock down the facility at five. Officer Jones will drive you back to Denver before then."

The walk from the conference room to the interview room involves three hallways and two security gates where Tony has to be buzzed through after showing his face to a camera on the ceiling. The halls are a cheerful lime green accented by an orange stripe in the center. The floors have two yellow lines which control the direction of foot traffic. He cannot see any guards on his brief walk, but is sure guards are watching his every move. His foot paces do not echo. The halls are silent. There it is—a large brown door marked *Interview Room Number 3*. The door is buzzed open. He enters, and sits to his left with his back to the mirrored wall.

"Sir, are you ready to start your interview?"

"Yes."

A minute of silence is broken by the buzzing and opening of the door to his right, and the escorted entry of KES. The very black, chiseled face woman stands erect before the table in an attempt to assume the alpha position. She looks down at Tony. The two escorting guards forcibly help her to sit in the chair facing Tony. The chair is bolted to the floor. Leg shackles force her to shuffle. Or is that a plea for sympathy. The guards lock her wrist shackles to the chair arms and leg shackles to the legs of the metal chair. Normal actions within an ultra-max prison.

"Good afternoon, my name is Tony Sattill. What shall I call you?"

After fifteen years, the dialog between cop and criminal is reopened.

"My name is Katherine Elizabeth Samuels, inmate number seven-five-nine-two-one-zero. Have we met before?"

"Yes, fifteen years ago, you and a group of men posing as your soldiers were arrested at the REACH Mission in New York City."

"Now I remember it and you well. Your lackey bitch beat me and dragged me in front of the cameras as if I were a prize animal she stalked and captured. She arrested me, while others hid in the background only to reappear at the kangaroo court you call the justice system. But I'm beyond all that. I'm not proud of my past. I only look to the present. The future will be built upon the present."

"Well, I'm happy to see you again, Ms. Samuels. If you're amenable, I'd like to ask you a few questions."

"Do I have a choice?"

"Yes, you can ask to go back to your cell, or you can stay here, and we can talk."

"I'll stay. You obviously need the company."

"First, let me ask if you have kept in touch with Mrs. Razdarovich and Mrs. Linder?"

"How would that be possible?"

"Well, you could send a letter to your lawyer, who would pass along your greetings to the women."

"You have my correspondence, and most likely transcripts of my telephone calls. You know what I have written and said. Did you find any references to those two crones?"

"No, I did not."

"Are you playing lawyer by asking questions for which you already have the answer in an effort to trick me or trip me in a lie? We'll get along better and this interview will be more productive if you ask questions for which only I have the answer."

"That's fair. No more trick questions. What was your involvement in the murders of Jamie Lanno, Thomas Clarkton, Joan Mussleman, and William Swarts?"

"None, I'm in prison. Contact with the outside world is limited to my family and my lawyer. I have no family. So I communicate, insofar as possible, with my attorney."

"Yes, I believe his name is Eliot Livingston."

"Correct."

"Are you aware of, or have any knowledge of, a motorcycle club named Archangels?"

"No, and why would I be associated with a gang of drug dealers?"

BINGO!

Tony didn't say associated. He said aware of or have any knowledge of. He said motorcycle club, and she said gang. He never mentioned drug dealing, she did. Very interesting leap of thought from question to response. Was that a mistake or was an intentional parry to his thrust? Did she slip or did she want Tony to know what he already knows? Tony is betting on the latter. The game of cat and mouse has begun in earnest. Two hours into the interview, they are still sparring over what may appear to be minutia. These facts will help Tony build his case against her and her cabal.

"Why did you dismiss your original attorney and hire Eliot Livingston?"

"Mr. Livingston was mentioned to me during the witch-hunt trial as a man who could get things done. But I ignored the opportunity. A few years ago, I saw the error of my ways—the error of not having an aggressive attorney to protect my rights. So I spoke to him and he seems to have developed several approaches to have me released. As you noted from my files, I have not been in any type of trouble for years. I'm being rehabilitated by the oppressive system. I learned how to deal with my anger and the frustration of losing everything to the system controlled by the white man."

Her anger is not totally under control. It is too deep seated.

"Are you familiar with Benny Radle, David Ellis, Wilson Abraham, or Ernest Davis?"

"No, who are they?"

"You may remember them as Betoto Magname, Ugata Nmbata, Dekena Rbille, and Nuta Breata. When they used their given names, they were in the mission's army."

"Now, I recall, vaguely, their names. But I've not seen or heard from them since the trial. Why do you ask?"

"It seems they changed their names about the same time that you changed yours, and I was wondering if it were a cause and effect or simple coincidence?"

"I can only assume coincidence."

"Why did you change your name?"

"I felt it would be better to shed the trappings of the old and try to accelerate my rehabilitation by Americanizing myself and blending in with the crowd."

"I see that Mr. Livingston has yet to visit you and all of your contact is either in letters or by telephone. Do you expect to see him before you file your appeal for release?"

She looks slightly stunned. A minor tell. "Mr. Livingston is working on the appeal process. He hopes to have papers filed in the next six months. I guess I'll see him when he's ready. He really doesn't need to see me until then. He has access to all the court documents on which an appeal must be based."

"Do you know the whereabouts of the aforementioned four men?"

"I assume they're still incarcerated."

"I know you know differently. I know that you know the men have been paroled after twelve years of fifteen-year sentences. I'm sure Mr. Livingston has informed you of this fact. I don't know how he provided the information, but I'm sure he did. I just wondered if you knew where the four men were living at this time."

"No."

Her anger resurfaces ever so slightly. This is a line of questioning Tony must pursue further.

"Would it surprise you to learn that two of the men live in the Bronx and two live in Northern New Jersey? Would it surprise you to know that David Ellis and Wilson Abraham are being sought for the murder of Lieutenant Jamie Lanno, who was the officer who cuffed you at the Mission? When we arrest them, will they tell us that they were doing your bidding?"

"Three questions, three answers. Yes. Yes. No."

"Why did you order the two men to butcher her womanhood? Was this some sort of clumsy message you wanted to broadcast? Clarkton had his tongue cut out, because he bragged about the arrest. Mussleman had her tongue cut out, because she was the voice of the people. Swarts had is eyes gouged out, because he was a key forensic accounting witness against you three ladies."

"While the three deaths are tragic and, as you described them, gruesome, I had nothing to do with the deaths. How could I? I'm locked up for twenty-two hours a day in a cell two thousand miles from New York City."

Tony never mentioned New York City. "One last question. Who's next on your hit list?"

"I do not have a hit list as you call it. I'm a prisoner, working hard in rehabilitation, not a puppeteer getting others to do my bidding."

"That's exactly what you are. You're a puppeteer queen sitting on a throne in a concrete fortress and dictating the actions of your minions. Thank you for your time today. It has been productive. I have learned a great deal. More than I could have hoped for. May the remainder of your life sentence go as well as the first decade."

"Thank you, Captain Sattill NYPD Retired. I hope your life and that of your family goes well also."

How well she played and threatened him. Just like a cat plays with a mouse before the death bite. At the airport and during the entire flight back to New York, the dread of real and present danger for Tony's family encases him.

Chapter 9

Friday nine a.m., two boney black men with large Afro hair styles, mustaches, and love patches walk briskly, but not at a panic pace, from the express platform of the East Side IRT lines. As they exit the station using the empty back stairs to the local platform, they remove and toss their dark gray coveralls. They rush up the stairs from the local platform to the Southwest corner of 86th Street and Lexington Avenue. They go unnoticed. They just blend into the late commuter crowd. The two men hail a cab and head south.

At nine-ten the first wisps of smoke appear on the express platform. Quickly wisps become small clouds of acrid blue-green smoke. Small clouds become billows from the brimstone of hell that burn the lungs and eyes of those waiting for an express train. Panic explodes. Those on the platform begin running for their lives, except they can't inhale enough oxygen to support running too far or up flights of stairs. Women are crying. Men are staggering about and cursing. Running evolves quickly into pushing—pushing anyone blocking the way of escape. The elderly and the infirmed are forced away from the escape path on the concrete platform. Several are knocked down. They become the speed bumps on the road to escape.

The downtown IRT Number Five train pulls to its stop and passengers rush to exit. They are immediately engulfed by the heavy suffocating smoke. Some passengers rush in the direction of the stairs to the local platform. Some attempt to get back on the train. The cloud follows them and begins to fill the cars. No one and nowhere are safe from the ominous cloud. The cacophony of agony creates further panic and more pushing to reach safety.

The conductor calls in an emergency fire notification. The East Side IRT express lines, uptown and downtown, are shut down immediately.

The yet-to-be riders standing on the local platform are witnesses to the cloud and those erupting from the express platform. Rapidly the smoke builds in the Number Four waiting area, and people ape those fleeing from the platform below. They panic and run to the exits. Once more screaming, pushing, and trampling are the norms. Civility is lost in this life-preservation mode. The Number Four pulls into the station and passengers exit. They are immediately engulfed by the heavy suffocating smoke. Some passengers rush in the direction of the stairs. Some attempt to get back on the train. The cloud follows them and begins to fill the cars. No one and nowhere are safe from the ominous cloud. The cacophony of agony creates further panic and more pushing to reach safety. Both the conductor and the MTA employee in the booth, call to the central dispatcher. The East Side IRT local line, uptown and downtown, is shut down.

People clog the exits. No one wants to be the last to leave or to be left behind in the smoke from hell. The intersection of 86th Street and Lexington Avenue is populated by riders seeking relief. Mary, the poor soul that begs for change and cries when it rains, is knocked over, and her sparsely-filled change bucket and sign, PLEASE HELP ME, spew onto the sidewalk. Most of the riders step over her. Some stumble on her.

People simply sit on the curb and try to regain their breathing rhythm. Several are puking and many are crying, rubbing their eyes, and spitting. In the distance police and ambulance sirens call out that rescue is in its way. Two partially blinded passengers wander into the street causing a cab to screech to a halt and be rear-ended by another taxi. No one rushes to help. The questions on everyone's lips are what, who, and why.

⌘⌘⌘

Friday nine-ten a.m., another two boney black men with large Afro hair styles, mustaches, and love patches walk briskly, but not at a panic pace from the express platform of the West Side IRT lines. As they exit the station using the empty back stairs to the local platform, they remove and toss their dark gray coveralls. They rush up the stairs from the local platform to the Southwest corner of 86th Street and Seventh Avenue. They go unnoticed. They just blend into the late commuter crowd. The two men hail a cab and head south.

At nine-twenty, the first wisps of smoke appear on the express platform. Quickly wisps become small clouds of acrid blue-green smoke. Small clouds become billows from the brimstone of hell that burn the lungs and eyes of those waiting for an express train. Panic explodes. Those on the platform begin running for their lives, except they can't inhale enough oxygen to support running too far or up flights of stairs. Women are crying. Men are staggering about and cursing. Running evolves quickly into pushing—pushing anyone blocking the way of escape. The elderly and the infirmed are forced away from the escape path on the concrete platform. Several are knocked down. They become the speed bumps on the road to escape.

The downtown IRT Number Two express train pulls to its stop and passengers rush to exit. They are immediately engulfed by the heavy suffocating smoke. Some passengers rush in the direction of the stairs to the local platform. Some attempt to get back on the train. The cloud follows them and begins to fill the cars. No one and nowhere are safe from the ominous cloud. The cacophony of agony creates further panic and more pushing to reach safety.

The conductor calls in an emergency fire notification. The West Side IRT express lines, uptown and downtown, are shut down immediately.

The yet-to-be riders standing on the local platform are witnesses to the cloud and those fleeing from the express platform. Rapidly, the smoke builds in the Number One waiting area, and people stare at those fleeing from the platform below them. They panic and run to the exits. Once more screaming, pushing, and trampling are the norms. Civility is lost in this life-preservation mode. The Number Two local pulls into the station and passengers exit. They are immediately engulfed by the heavy suffocating smoke. Some passengers rush in the direction of the stairs. Some attempt to get back on the train. The cloud follows them and begins to fill the cars. No one and nowhere are safe from the ominous cloud. The cacophony of agony creates further panic and more pushing to reach safety. Both the conductor and the MTA employee in the booth, call to the central dispatcher. The West Side IRT local line, uptown and downtown, is shut down.

People clog the exits. No one wants to be the last to leave or to be left behind in the smoke from hell. The intersection of 86th Street and Seventh Avenue is populated by riders seeking relief. Jimmy MacInerny, on his way to his violin lesson, is pushed against the wall of the platform. His violin falls to the ground. As he bends over to retrieve his most prize possession, he and it are crushed by a herd of men in moderately expensive suits, who were on their way to important business meetings. Most of the riders thereafter step over Jimmy. Some stumble on him.

People simply sit on the curb and try to regain their breathing rhythm. Several are puking and many are crying, rubbing their eyes, and spitting. In the distance, police and ambulance sirens call out that rescue is on its way. Two partially blinded passengers wander into the street, causing a cab to screech to a halt and be rear-ended by another taxi. No one rushes to help. The questions on everyone's lips are what, who, and why?

∽∾∽

Friday nine-fifty a.m. the guards and other employees of Friendly Neighborhood Bank on the corner of Seventh Avenue and 29th Street are making preparations for the delivery of cash from the downtown depository. This is a "double day," a Friday which is also the fifteenth of the month. More money than usual will be delivered to this bastion of the garment industry. Normal weekly delivery is $150,000. But this day, $250,000 will be delivered. Employees want to cash their paychecks. Owners and partners want to replenish their safes and strong boxes. Numerous special envelopes will be filled and delivered to men who don't work in the garment industry, but who are silent partners. These men appear every two weeks, accept the envelopes, and leave in stretch limos. No one questions them or their reasons for being.

Half way down the block on the side opposite the bank and in a position to head south is a dark blue van with a woman in the driver's seat. On the bank's side of the street in a position to head around the corner is a steel gray SUV with another woman in the driver's seat.

Four bald boney black men sit in the Thread and Needle Coffee shop enjoying breakfast. Their soft tones are broken by an occasional burst of muffled laughter. They periodically check out the van and SUV as they glance through the large front window.

Around the corner of 29th and 7th lumbers the Spartan Services armored truck. As it eases to a stop in front of the bank, three large men approach their soon-to-be personal ATM. The guard on the passenger's side leaps out and sprints to the rear of the armored, the door opens, and a third guard lifts a dolly out of the truck and a large canvas satchel to the open door way. The guard from the passenger side loads the satchel onto a dolly and turns toward the bank.

Immediately, the three large men pull back their raincoats, cover their faces with Richard Nixon masks and brandish AK-47s. One masked man goes to the driver's side, inserts the muzzle of the automatic weapon into the conversation hole in the door and fires a burst of eight rounds. The driver is bounced around in the cab like a rag doll. Blood splatters throughout the cab. Simultaneously, a second masked man delivers eight to ten rounds into each of the other two guards. The third masked man empties the banana clip of the AK-47 into the front ends and tires of the street traffic, thus causing a complete road jam. He replaces the clip and empties the second one about six feet above the heads of the pedestrians on both sidewalks and demands that they lie down.

The four black men rise from the booth, pay their tab and leave a twenty-dollar tip. The tab was $22.50 tab. They exit the coffee shop just as the three masked men commence shooting. Two of the men run to and retrieve the satchel. They take the satchel to the dark blue van where they are joined by the other two. The three masked men run to the SUV. The SUV and van screech away from their parking spots and head in opposite directions.

☙❧☙

All security forces are on hyper mode. The Transit police cordon off the East Side and West Side 86th Street IRT Stations. Hazmat clad inspectors and the bomb squad with all its electronic devices are in the stations trying to determine the cause and severity of the attack. There are six EMTs wagons at each site. The yellow police tape is triple wrapped around the exit area where people are gathered. No is allowed one in and no one is allowed out. The police and SWAT teams have created a ten block perimeter around each station. The canvassing has started. TV and radio stations have sent teams that must stay behind the yellow tape and wait to talk to those affected by the attack.

☙❧☙

The squad cars made a perfect V at both ends of the 28th-29th Street block, thus containing the bank, the armored truck and a hundred or so terrified citizens. They had to secure the crime scene before the EMS wagons could get to the slaughtered guards. The use of gunfire requires it. A few people had fled, but most stayed to be part of the investigation and to be seen on the news.

‿♋‿

"This is News Breaker Nine, Your Source for All That Matters.

"We go live to the borough of Manhattan where there have been two nearly simultaneous attacks on subway riders. We say two attacks—one at the West Eighty-Sixth Street Station of the IRT and one at the East Eighty-Sixth Street Station of the IRT. Our reporter on the East Side Stephanie Snyder. Stephanie, what can you tell us?"

"Between nine and nine-thirty, people waiting for an East Side IRT train, noticed blue-green acrid smoke roiling up from the express platform. They scrambled to escape the threat and exited onto the intersection of Eighty-Sixth Street and Lexington Avenue. We have not yet spoken to the Fire Chief in charge and the Emergency Medical staff about injuries. The police have not released the train passengers and those waiting for trains for us to interview. What we can see and hear are many people coughing, crying and spitting. Apparently the smoke has caused substantial irritation to their eyes and respiratory system. We have been informed that both uptown and downtown lines have been shut down until the Police say otherwise. Captain, Captain Johnson: What can you tell your fellow New Yorkers about the attack on the IRT subway riders?"

"We're currently investigating the severity of the damage to both human life and property. We have several investigators from our Hazardous Materials squad down on the platform and the tunnels. They're trying to determine the cause of the smoke, and whether it's dangerous or noxious. That's all I can say at this time. Now if you'll excuse me I have work to coordinate. We anticipate making a statement of our findings within forty-five minutes. Thank you."

"For now, this is Stephanie Snyder at the Lexington Avenue IRT Eight-Sixth Street Station."

🙠🙢

"News Eleven. Your World in Real Time.

"We interrupt our regularly scheduled programming to bring you an on the spot report from Seventh Avenue between Twenty-Eighth and Twenty-Ninth Streets. There has been a robbery of an armored truck and the murder of the three guards. Live on the scene is Brent Tucker. Brent, what can you tell our viewers?"

"News Eleven has learned that the robbery and shoot out occurred in front of the Friendly Neighborhood Bank about ten a.m. It seems that the armored truck from Spartan Services was about to deliver a large supply of cash to the bank. Just as the guards opened the back door and prepared to take the bag of money into the bank, large and masked men, armed with automatic weapons, rushed them. We're not sure how many masked gunmen there were. Some accounts tell us three and some say five. The driver and two guards were gunned down in a hail of fire. The gunmen then turned their weapons on the cars in the street creating several accidents and the people on the sidewalks causing great panic. Then several black men ran into the street and grabbed the bag of money and carried it to a large blue vehicle. Some bystanders say an SUV, some say a van. This vehicle headed south. The masked gunmen got into a pick-up truck or SUV. The color of which is white or silver. They headed around the corner. The police arrived about three minutes after the shooting ended. Someone or several people in the crowd used their cell phones to call the police. As the police talk to the people on the sidewalks and those in the cars and taxis, they're determining if anyone filmed the shoot out and robbery. We'll stay on the scene to interview the bystanders. This is Brent Tucker on Seventh Avenue between Twenty-Eighth and Twenty-Ninth Streets, reporting on a vicious murder and bank robbery. Back to the studio."

⸮⸿⸮

"This is Investigator Eight. The Truth Seeker.

"We go live to the West Eighty-Sixth Street IRT stop in Manhattan where there has been a gas and smoke attack on subway riders. Our reporter on the scene is Mandy Johns. Mandy, what can you tell us?"

"Between nine and nine-thirty, people waiting for a West Side IRT train, noticed blue-green acrid smoke coming up from the express platform. The smoke quickly billowed onto the local platform. Passengers and those awaiting a train scrambled to escape the threat and exited onto the intersection of Eighty-Sixth Street and Seventh Avenue. Right now the fire department and the emergency medical staff are working feverishly to help the injured. When they're released, we'll interview several IRT riders. What we can see and hear are many people coughing, crying, and wandering around aimlessly. Apparently, the smoke has caused substantial irritation to their eyes and respiratory system. We've been informed that both uptown and downtown lines have been shut down until the Police say otherwise. Captain, Captain Laine: What can you tell your fellow New Yorkers about the attack on the IRT subway riders?"

"We're currently investigating the severity of the damage to both human life and property. We have several investigators from our Hazardous Materials squad down on the platform and the tunnels. They're trying to determine the cause of the smoke, and whether it is dangerous or noxious. That's all I can say at this time. Now if you'll excuse me, I have to make sure everyone is taken care of and that we get statements. We anticipate making a statement of our findings within forty-five minutes. Thank you."

"For now, this is Mandy Johns at the Eighty-Sixth Street IRT Seventh Avenue Station."

ဢჄჀ

The blue van heads south to the Holland Tunnel. The woman drives carefully, but not so slow as to attract attention. On the New Jersey side, she pays the toll. The four black men sit patiently. The vehicle exits the road complex and heads toward a landfill—a grave yard of unwanted cars, trucks, vans, and people, who simply disappeared. There the driver, passengers, and canvas satchel are transferred to an F-150 Lariat model. They exit the landfill. Eight minutes later, an explosion and fire ball can be heard and seen from the New Jersey Turnpike.

The steel gray SUV travels east across Manhattan and south to Brooklyn. Then onto the Brooklyn-Queens Expressway toward a club house in an alley.

ဢჄჀ

The panic and paranoia in Manhattan are at epic levels. All exit roads are barricaded and entry or exit requires identification. No subways or busses will run until they can be checked by the bomb squad. All Long Island Railroad or New York Central trains are stopped where they stand. Every underground station is patrolled by bomb sniffing dogs. The police are in full riot gear. Concern about Martial Law is raised by the Mayor. Life appears to be grinding to a halt. But the bars and restaurants are filled to capacity, and Manhattan residents fight for taxis to get home. Or they walk however far it is to their brownstone or apartment. It is, after all New York, and it is spring, the season of promise.

Chapter 10

Brendan, can you conference in Chris? We all need to know what the fuck happened and what is going to happen."

"Tony, this is Chris. Here's what I know and what I suspect about the subway attacks. My source at the bomb squad tells me the devices that were used were simple, crude, and effective—and both subway events were initiated by the similar devices. The core of the concept is a two dish hot plate like the ones to keep coffee hot in the squad room. The hot plate was powered by a battery pack. It was placed in a trash basket on the express level. It was laid on a stack of newspapers, and two gallon paint cans were placed on the heating surfaces. One can contained bleach and one can contained ammonia. When the hot plate was turned on the heat began to cook the liquids and the paper around the device. The paper smoldered then burned, while the bleach and ammonia boiled. The fumes from the boiling liquids merged with the paper smoke. The merged liquids' fumes became a compound similar to the fumes of hydrochloric acid.

"These same fumes inhaled in substantial volume,

will burn the membrane in a person's throat, erode the little hair-like filters in the lungs, and cause extensive coughing and mucus rejection. If this situation is not treated immediately, the person who has inhaled the large volume of fumes will go into respiratory arrest. They will cease to breathe normally and die an agonizing death. However, given the placement of the smoke bomb, the slowness of the heat generation, the large size of the space to be filled—thousands of cubic feet of space—and the fact that the smoke rose above peoples' heads, there was little danger of death. Just massive amounts of discomfort and panic. The investigators believe those were the desired effects.

"Cameras on the two platforms have recorded the same thing; two boney black men leaving the area in which each device was found. These men had large Afro hair styles, mustaches, and love patches. Obviously not afraid to be seen. They wore dark gray coveralls as if they were workmen. Each two man set was seen on camera exiting the respective stations. One set had already removed their coveralls. These were found on the local level. The second set of coveralls was found in a trash basket outside the West Side station. The crime lab is now checking DNA on all four coveralls."

"Brandon, what have you learned?"

"Guys, the robbery and murder of the armored truck guards were well executed and brutal. All of it was caught on the security cameras around the bank. I'm intrigued by the fact that four boney black men appear to have been working with three large masked men armed with AK-Forty-Sevens. I see a direct connection between the Ethiopians and the Archangels. I suspect the Archangels wanted to bring their home bank account back up to one million dollars after the police helped themselves to a bunch of their money. So, I'm curious—why now and why that amount? Why a million? It must be that the big drug deal we heard about is about to go down. The police are checking DNA and finger prints on the spent cartridges for matches in the system."

"Tony, Chris and I believe the subway events were diversions to attract the police away from the robbery of the armored truck. The money was the objective of the day, and no one has found the three masked men or four black men—or the vehicles they used for escape."

"I agree. I'll relay all of these facts and suspicions to Commander Vincent so he can pass them down the chain of command and get some credit, while we stay out of the limelight. We must wait while the wheels of law enforcement truth grind ponderously forward. Guys, I think we've done all we can do for now. I'm going away on the three-day lecture junket, the week after next. I leave on Sunday and will be back Wednesday night. Just in time for Bartheleme's acting debut. Until then let's lay low. If I haven't said it before, you guys are the best. Talk in ten days."

✒✑✒✑

"Dad, did you hear what happened at the subway station? A big explosion and fire."

"I heard two people were killed in the blast."

"Hundreds of people had to go to the ER."

"Children, relax and let me tell you really what happened."

Tony's mostly sanitized version seems to disappoint his three offspring. There is nothing duller than the boring adult factual truth, because there is no fantasy. The two boys and Cassandra head for their rooms, crestfallen.

"Dinner in fifteen minutes. Carmelita made all the fixings for tacos. Now big bad policeman, tell me really what happened at the two subway stations."

"During dinner clean up, sweetie."

Watching the three teens inhale their food gives Tony the idea of giving them family-only nicknames—Hoover, Electrolux, and Oreck. He tells Melissa, who agrees the children's food consumption demeanor is unbecoming but ardently discourages the renaming of her offspring. She will talk to them. Tony then tells Melissa all he has told Commander Vincent. Which is not everything.

"Why do you think these two disparate groups are connected?"

"We have reason to believe that a big drug buy is about to occur. The Archangels are the main point of purchase, and I believe the four Ethiopians will act as go betweens the Archangels and the street dealers. The total buy of meth and heroin of one million dollars could result in a total gross of well over five million dollars. The Archangels would get at least three million dollars and the Ethiopians would get one million dollars. The rest would be distributed among the fifty to seventy-five street dealers.

"I believe the Ethiopians could use their cut to reestablish their empire of international drug dealing, gun running, and money laundering. Similar to what they ran fifteen years ago. Hell, it's all they know, and the sources for the money and drugs are still around. The Mexicans always need a way to launder their ill-gotten gains, and the Russians always need to sell weapons to the rebels of the world. All they need is money from someone to pay for the weapons. I think the Archangels are in the game for the money to expand their empire in this country. They want more territory to sell more drugs to get richer to expand into more territory. Commander Vincent is aware of my suspicions and he has alerted the DEA and our own Narco Cops. These two groups will handle all the investigation and logistics from here on out. Chris, Brendan, and I can return to our normal lives with no fear of violence."

"Tony, this sounds just like it was before the children, except now there're children and us. And you're not a cop any longer."

"That's why I turned over all this information to Commander Vincent. Let him get the credit. Let the precinct captains and the narco squad do all the heavy lifting. Chris, Brendan, and I were just shadow soldiers. We're now out of it completely. The bad guys will now focus on the drug buy and distribution, and the police will focus on stopping the transfer of money for drugs. I'm done. Although I still want to get the bastards that killed Jamie, I'm now out of it until that time. Until such time as the Ethiopians are captured. Then I want in on the trial. You and the children are safe."

"Should I still carry my gun?"

"No, and I'll tell Adolfo that he can transport the children as usual. You're free to take taxis and go about your business. I'll call the school and the building management. You talk to Carmelita. Now, does the hard-working retired captain get a little sugar for his efforts?"

"He might, if he pours me a brandy and rubs my back after the children are asleep."

"Gawd, what onerous tasks you put me through."

☙❧

Once in his chair in the solarium, Tony sees a ten-inch stack of very colorful and enticing brochures for summer camps. On top of the stack is a note: *Read. Let's discuss with the children. Decision time is upon us!*

Melissa has grouped the brochures by child. Each grouping contains people, places, and things to enrich and enhance each child's bent with six weeks of nearly single-minded activity from dawn to dusk. Sports camps for Antonio, theater camps for Bartheleme, and science camps for Cassandra.

Each camp is "ideally suited" for gifted children ages twelve through seventeen. The campers look oh-so-happy. The counselors look oh-so-attractive and healthy. The settings are oh-so-bucolic and clean. It is almost as if Melissa is trying to trying to plumb the depth of commitment of each child into his or her particular field. How deep will the child delve before the child decides that this is what he or she wants out of life or that he or she has had enough and wants nothing more to do with this activity. It's like the SEAL boot camp. Some will make it and some will crash and burn. Tony thinks of the possibility of emotional damage. Not a pretty prospect for his three.

There is a fourth group of brochures depicting a smattering of educational activities, such as history, biology, botany, geology, carpentry, farming, and animal husbandry. There is also many outdoor programs and events, such as soccer, basketball, swimming, nature walks, overnight hikes, and trust and confidence courses.

All the camps are coed. It is an interesting concept—a group of pre-and sub-teens chaperoned by a group of young adults, who are not parents of the campers. The younger group is in the initial stages of hormone overload and away from their real parents for nearly two months. Children ages twelve to seventeen love to explore. Maybe members of the opposite sex. This type of education could be dangerous. All the camps are located in Western Massachusetts, Vermont, or New Hampshire. No more than a three hour drive from Manhattan. And each camp has a four-day parent's weekend over July fourth.

Tony thinks that summer camps were created to:

A. Give kids a break from the big bad cities
B. Give kids a break from their parents
C. Give parents a break from their children
D. Let children explore geography foreign to their own
E. Teach children totally useless crafts
F. Teach children about poisonous snakes and venomous spiders
G. Teach children how to make and eat s'mores
H. Let children explore their inner self
I Let children learn self-reliance
J. Teach children how to do laundry
K. Teach children to live in a community of peers
L. Expose children to institutional food
M. Expose children to different social groups

Of all the offerings, the Putney Farm in Vermont gets Tony's vote. As an extension of the children's school, it is not a boot camp. Likely, most of the other children at the camp also attend the Day School. Many of the counselors are also teachers at the school. So, there won't be many new faces or attitudes to disrupt the summer transition. On the down side, this may be restrictive to their social growth. On the upside, there is a built-in comfort zone.

The camp is a working farm with baseball, soccer, and volleyball teams that play other camps; has a complete science lab; and puts on two shows—one for the parents on July fourth and one for the campers/farmers at the end of the session. Tony knows his vote is only one of three—the children must vote as one. Melissa's parliamentary rules are convoluted, but they are the rules. Camp will be the topic for dinner.

The next letter is the quarterly statement of interest and dividends spun off from his portion of the City Employee Pension. The to be deposited into Tony's checking account this Friday the amount will cover a portion of the children's summer camp costs and leave enough for Melissa's Mother's Day gift—an antique gold lace ring from Buccellati. Is there ever enough?

The next stack of mail is comprised of junk and bills. Tony is never sure which is which. Sleep overcomes him slowly.

His power nap lasts forty-five minutes. Time for a cup of coffee and the papers. The *Times* and the *Ledger* carry comments from eye-witnesses and release that is not to look like a release from the NYPD—a quote from an anonymous source in the department. Each newspaper carries artist recreations of what the eyewitnesses can remember, as well as photos lifted from security cameras in all three locations. Each newspaper has its own anonymous source, yet each source says the same things and uses the same phrases.

The department believes that the subway incidents were decoys to divert police attention from the armored truck robbery. The police believe because of this and numerous other factors, the total crime was committed by a very professional gang. The gang is made up of both black and white men. They have several leads, which are being pursued in earnest. If anyone has any information about the subway incidents, the armored truck robbery, and the murder of the three guards, the public is advised to call 800-hot-tips. Spartan Services is offering a $50,000 reward payable upon the capture of the murderers. The name of any caller will be held in the strictest confidence

Buried on the inside pages of the newspapers is a little blurb—eight lines long, mentioning a break-in and robbery at the Brooklyn Army Depot. A vehicle and several weapons appear to be missing. The MPs and local police are investigating.

Lunch time, then off to see Antonio team play St Bernard's JVs.

The Day School JV Baseball team is six and three going into the last two weeks of the season. If they win the next two games, they could tie for the top spot in the unofficial league. Still, Tony is one of only three adult males in the stands. There are only five adult females. The balance of the sparse crown is comprised of the players' peers. Antonio is unaware of Tony's presence until he hears the familiar whistle. A shrill call that announces "Dad is here." Tony's father taught Tony the whistle, because it was valuable for calling children, taxis, and dogs. When he hears his father's pronouncement, Antonio turns, looks into the bleachers, stands straight, and raises his arm. A young macho acknowledgment of respect.

The first two innings are meaningless—infield grounders, pop flies, and strike outs. Antonio is beginning to master the sprint down to first base behind or beside the batter who has hit an infield grounder. An exhausting requisite for the position. Top of the third, the very fast St. Bernard second baseman bunts the ball. It rolls slowly toward the third baseman. Antonio jumps up like a cat come alive and pounces on the ball like as if it were a slow mouse. He turns and throws a rope to the first baseman. Out by six feet. The bench goes wild and Antonio gets high fives from all including the coach.

In the bottom of the third, Antonio swings way too late on three fastballs. Fatigue is showing. Nothing of consequence in the fourth and fifth innings. St. Bernard scratches out a run in the top of the final inning. Two singles and a sacrifice fly to deep center. In the bottom of the sixth the Day School gets nothing. Heads fall as the team gathers up the tools of the trade and wends its way to the bus.

෨෬෨

The light blue Varnon Trucking eighteen-wheeler heads west but does not use any Interstate or toll roads and thus avoids the weighing and inspections that are required on those two paths. Reaching the destination will take an extra three days by using "off" routes, but the truck's cargo will be safe from prying eyes. The three large men in the cab take six hour driving shifts. The ten passengers inside the truck, four black and six white, sleep as best they can. The box contains a vehicle, numerous boxes of army weapons and munitions, and mattresses. Before they left New York, the men purchase two RPGs and a box of grenades. These are their new toys. There are no lights in the big box except for hand held flash lights. Food, fuel, and bathroom stops are at six-hour intervals. The semi is followed by two silver-gray SUVs, each with a full passenger load. This caravan and its contents have a single purpose. Everyone is laser focused.

෨෬෨

The clamor of the children arriving home reflects their relief that the dark cloud of danger has been lifted from their lives. Carmelita has prepared roasted pork, yellow rice and black beans with flan for dessert. She waits for the arrival of the thundering herd, and gives each of them a hug, a kiss, and a sugar cookie with their name on it. She is near tears of joy as she leaves. No sense to tell the children not to eat the sugar cookie before dinner because it might spoil their appetites. Hell, a dinner before dinner would not spoil the appetites of these three happy noisy teens. Dinner is served.

"Tonight, we have to talk about what you'll be doing this summer. Your father and I think that summer camp would be a great idea. We've collected several brochures for each of you. Sports camps for Antonio, theater camps for Bartheleme, and science camps for Cassandra."

"Yuck."

The response is universal.

"Mom, what about Putney? I hear it's way cool. It's a farm with boating and the sports teams that play other camps."

"Plus, my science teacher will be there"

"They put on a musical for the parents and drama for the campers. And it's in Vermont. I hear it's beautiful. You guys could come up for the Fourth of July Parents' Weekend."

"We vote for Putney."

"Then it's unanimous. Your father and I are very happy all of you want to go to the same camp. Now homework."

The avalanche of positive attitude is heartwarming.

಄಄಄

"Tony, thank goodness, they made up our minds for us. Now all I have to worry about is getting them appropriately outfitted."

"Sweetie, I'll bet the school has a list of necessary items. And items that are not allowed like guns and dynamite. Let's contact the school first. Then we'll ask each of them what they would like to take. Because the children take after their minimalist father so much, I'll bet they won't want many extra items."

"I'll take that bet. Have you not noticed the way they get and keep things of seemingly no value other than sentimental? Watcha say to what I believe you police types call a yard?"

"You're on. A Benjamin it is, woman."

Chapter 11

Three footlockers are ordered from LL Bean. Tony buys three cell phones, which will be preprogrammed with the numbers for Tony, Melissa, home, grandparents, and each other. These will be presented and explained two days before departure.

Tony has to spend time prepping for the lecture circuit. He alters his presentation depending on the audience and the issues facing the specific police department. Different slides for different cops.

Tony's Crime Analysis Team (CAT) had its own way of addressing the crime scene. While these may not be directly applicable to each situation, they provide a few general guidelines. Each CAT includes a lead detective, a uniform, and two members from the Scientific and Technical Analysis Group. The STAGs are the lab rats, techies and near-meds.

Each member of the squad is assigned various aspects of the crime scene—one member details everything within ten yards of the victim's body, one member details everything outside that ring to the farthest impediment, such as a wall, up to fifty yards. Sniper hits require that the third member of the squad, most likely the lead detective, explore and detail the shooter's location. The CAT program is designed to train up-and-coming force members with actual crime scene procedure and analysis, as well as take the burden of initial data gathering off the shoulders of the investigative force.

CAT is headed by a young detective selected after rigorous psychological testing. Selected on the basis that the detective has all the right tools for command decisions and the gift of deep comprehension, for seeing the little details and their connections that abound at the scene or for sensing what is missing or what does not fit. For grasping what probably happened at a crime scene. Not the why, but the what. The lead detective is not a glamorous profiler. He or she is just a very observant, intelligent, and sensitive individual. The lead detective must be able to think like the killer, by getting into the killer's head via the information left at the scene of the crime.

CAT is the second call made in immediately discovered crimes. When the information is fresh, CAT can do good work. CAT also operates non-immediate violent crime situations—deaths, which are over twelve hours old. The trail of the perp is cold. Here is where CAT can do its best work—work that untrained detectives or patrolmen would not be able to complete effectively. CAT replaces the two detectives, four uniforms and a complete Crime Scene Unit in these cold situations only. Most calls for CAT come directly to the precinct and not through 911.

Veteran detectives sometimes hate the CAT squad because they think it takes the entire process of old-fashioned detective work away from the ill-fitting suits. What they really object to is that it is the crest of the wave of the future, wherein there will be greater specialization and greater reliance on awareness and sensitivity and less on legwork and the third degree. While the dinosaur is not yet extinct, the species is ill. The future, according to the seers and knowers, will be one of modularity. Each module will be connected by and interlinked to each other and the precincts are linked to each other via the citywide computer system. The entire plan is quite simple and very efficient. CAT is assembled and sent to the crime scene based on who is up: who is available from the various disciplines. A roster is kept in the department's main computer system and can be tapped by any precinct captain or shift commander. Often the team will be comprised of members who are not from the same precinct. The CATs are sent city-wide and not beholden to an individual precinct.

The team goes to the crime scene to gather all the pertinent information by spending time walking and looking at the scene from all angles, making observations, and drawing vague, but well documented conclusions, and issuing hypotheses. The four members speak into personal digital-recorders at the scene. Later they download electronic blips into networked laptops so they can read each other's findings and observations.

It's up to the team leader to merge and purge the information, infuse his hypotheses, and develop a single comprehensive report on the murder scene. This report along with the coroner's report is turned over to the investigating detectives within twenty-four hours of the on-site analysis. Addenda from anyone other than the Medical Examiner's office are considered a sign of shoddy work on the part of the CAT leader. An addendum is considered an error by the older detectives and corroborates their view that CAT is worthless. Many of MOs of the murder will not to be found in anyone's files. Thus, the critical nature of analyzing the crime scene, and the importance of the CAT squad.

Occam's Razor is the principle of simplicity. Among all the theories pertaining to a situation, the theory that contains or requires the fewest hypotheses is the most often the correct one. The principal has been restated to be the most obvious theory is the correct one. Most murders are committed by someone close to the victim—a relative or friend. This is an historic fact and meets the criteria of Occam's Razor. Therefore, close associates must be the first people sought for thorough questioning. This is the job of the riding or lead detective. Not the CAT squad.

If, after exhaustive probing and alibi checking, close associates and family are eliminated from the suspect pool, it may be advisable to consider Tony Sattill's Principal of the Other Side of the Coin. Clues and information from the crime scene provide only the visible side of the event. Consider the event to be a coin. What is on the other side, may be the perp. Not all murders are committed by men. Not all robberies are for money only. Not all kidnappings are for extortion. Sometimes the perp is an associate of the police or a detective and not the victim.

Tony is confident that his presentation will produce many questions about process, procedures, and people. All asked by local police officers who have specific issues to resolve.

⌒⌒⌒

The plane from LaGuardia lands smoothly at Denver International Airport. As the herd of passengers exits, a slightly built, short, well-dressed man, with dark ringlets on his collar walks casually to the Ground Transportation hub. His Banty cloths and demeanor are out of place in this airport. His eyes are constantly darting left and right.

A taxi takes the man to the Motel 6 located on the eastern edge of the city.

The neighborhood is neither urban chic nor suburban. More likely referred to as next to rural. He has a reservation under the name of Benjamin Dover. His driver's license and VISA card confirm his identity. Once inside his room, he unpacks his sparse belongings and removes five pieces of plastic that were hidden within his carry-on case. He carefully assembles the pieces to a small .45 caliber hand gun. This he places in his attaché case inside and manila folder beneath three other folders. The cartridges for the gun are safe inside him.

He must make a phone call to confirm that the plane will be at the appointed location at the appointed time—two critical factors in the next phase of the process. Time and place are confirmed. Passenger load of the plane is confirmed. The payment of $200, 000 due before take-off is confirmed. Destination is confirmed. He calls destination. A plane, a substantial jet, at the first stop is confirmed, as is the second payoff, due in advance, of $200,000.

His next call is local and alerts a key party that everything is in motion for the drive into the dessert thirty-six hours from now, eight-thirty a.m. He must wait for the telephone call from the truck driver. That will signal the next phase of the process.

The call is greatly anticipated as is the ultimate payday. He is hungry for a big steak and few frosty beers. On his way into the motel, he noticed a western saloon next door to the motel. Perfect.

He changes from his traveling suit into a freshly starched white shirt, pressed jeans, and tasseled Cole & Haan loafers. Western chic.

❧❧❧

The large blue overland truck lumbers along, eighteen hours from Denver. Inside the truck the stench of body odor and some human waste lies heavy, while tempers are short. The blacks and whites have divided the big box into separate territories. Childish behavior from ten bored alpha males. The silver-gray SUVs, just as crowded, smell no sweeter, but the passengers are cordial. When all arrive in Denver, they will have a few hours to eat cooked food and bathe.

ℰℐℰℐ

The music from the four-piece band is loud and somewhat jarring to the stranger's New York ears. The most energetic music his ears are used to was written by Renaissance composers like Vivaldi and Albinoni. The steak is large and somewhat chewy. The beer is cold. The waitress flirts a tad too much. As evidenced by her stare and the obvious exposure of cleavage. His belly and his ego are becoming engorged.

"Ya'll done, friend?"

"With the food, yes. But I'll switch to scotch. Please get me the check. Will it be all right if I stay at the table and just enjoy the atmosphere?"

"Sure. Atmosphere? Where are you from anyway?"

"New York."

"New York. Shoot, we don' get many, if any, people from New York. They usually stay closer to downtown where all the touristy nightlife and sightseeing are. But you're dressed like a tourist. So what brings you to our neighborhood?"

On a blind self-dare, he responds with a smile and a flirtatious brush of his hand against her arm. "You."

"Well, I like your style. The band has finished its last set. Closing in one hour. I'm done with my shift and would like to join you for a drink and some pleasant conversation, if that's okay?

"I'm not going anywhere without you."

Having tipped her twenty-five dollars, the man is sure she will return. The bar does not carry an acceptable single malt scotch, so he selects Johnny Walker Red—a double with two ice cubes. He sips slowly, awaiting her return. In fifteen minutes, she bounces up to his table. She is all smiles. Her hair is down and the curls cascade on her shoulders. Her third blouse button is open, and she has the scent of perfume found on the second shelf of a drug store.

"What would you like to drink?" he asks.

"Jack neat."

"Allow me to wait on you."

He returns with a double Jack.

"Thank you, kind sir. Now tell me all about yourself. Start with your name. Mine is Annalee."

Mr. Benjamin Dover spins a web of lies and half-truths as to his raison d'être. Annalee is enthralled.

"Now what about you, Annalee?"

Divorced from a piece-of-shit truck driver, who screwed anything that wore a skirt, except her, even when he was drunk, she lives in a trailer with her three dogs. She is waiting tables and shooing away the locals until she can get out of town. One year of community college completed and one more in the works. Majoring in graphic design. Then she is gone to LA or 'Frisco to find a better life. Her second Jack slows down her speech. Her eyes are glassy. His second Red, fuels his desire. The conversation wends its way through relationships, his job, and her future. Thrice during the conversation, she leans into his space, touching his arm and forcing her blouse to open as fully as possible to expose her breasts. She whispers seductively, while he talks in a low tone. Always the alpha male, he is in control. The lights in the saloon flicker off and on to bright. The evening is over for patrons and employees.

"Well, Annalee, we're being thrown out. Are you able to drive safely?"

"I'm not sure. This cowgirl may need a soft place to lay her head before she heads home."

The cat and mouse game changes levels.

"Well, I'm staying at Motel Six. I'll bet they have a room available. Why don't we walk over and find out? I don't think it's a good for you to be driving in your condition. Which car is yours?"

"Yes, let us go to your motel. To your room. My blue Malibu is parked behind the bar. It'll be there in the morning."

She heads out the door, six feet in front of him. Her steps are unsteady, and she leans on him when they are outside. Then she turns, and her lips attack his face. The hunger in her mouth comes from too many nights alone and angry. His arousal is near apex.

Their pace quickens back to his motel room. Upon closing the door, they clutch and grab and grope. His hands find the right buttons on her blouse and jeans, while hers find the belt, fly button, and zipper of his pants. She is on the floor before him, trying to inhale his manhood. It, like the man, is undersized, but it is as hard as teak wood, and she is drunk. He takes her by the shoulders and pulls her to an erect position. They stagger their way across the floor and the strewn cloths to the bed. He pulls off his pants and the bed cover just before she flops like so much dead meat onto the bed. She is naked. She raises her knees to display a bald mons.

"Now you do me while I do you. Then we can do it."

How quaint, he thinks as he straddles her and buries his face in her precious parts, while she takes him in her mouth, again. Her orgasm is reached in a few minutes. She is a howler. He is yet to reach nirvana.

"Come inside me now," she commands.

Her raised thighs provide perfect guides for his approach. The forceful entry causes her to moan deeply as if years of frustration are being emitted. She clutches him fervently. Digs her fingers and short nails into his back. Her kisses are so opened mouth that he barely feels lips, just teeth and palate. The thrusting and pounding are in synch. Her moans and groans are moving up the octave. He is grunting like an animal. The activity has become frenetic. Sweat is another exchanged bodily fluid. As they approach bliss simultaneously. He stops and withdraws.

"What the hell are you doing? Are you done? I'm not. I want to get off again."

"I'm not done, and you'll get off again, we both will. I just want you to do something for me."

"What more can I do?"

"Wrap your hands around my neck and slowly apply choking pressure as we fuck."

"What the hell?"

"Erotic auto-asphyxiation heightens the experience. It's called EA, and it's not fatal. It makes my climax feel like ten climaxes all at once. You release your hands when I tell you. It will be safe. Trust me, this is not the first time I've done this."

"Okay, if you're sure."

He reinserts and the bouncing recommences at a slower rhythm. With the acceleration of their coupling, he takes her hands, places them around his neck, and squeezes them around his throat. The faster the action, the tighter she squeezes. Then it starts. At the base of his spine a sharp pulsating release begins to travel upward. Her hands are tight and the pulsing in his spine has become a pounding in his brain. Then bliss. Cosmic orgasmic bliss as he pulls her hands away and spews himself inside of her. The pounding and pulsing subside, his breathing returns to panting, and he collapses on the bed to her left. After two minutes his basic respiratory function is back to normal.

"That was fantastic. See I told you it would not be dangerous. My climax was so intense. It felt like I had never experienced it before. You should try it. You have nothing to lose. I'll stop when you tell me to."

"Okay. I'll try it. But when I say stop, you stop."

"Yes, indeed."

"Can you go again so soon?"

"That is an extra benefit of EA. I'm as ready as if I had not yet started."

"Okay, cowboy, git on and ride."

Again they commence the horizontal dance of lust. His hands are loosely around her neck.

"Okay so far, Annalee?"

"Okay, giddyup. The bucking bronco wants it all."

She enjoys this new experience. His tender kisses mixed with the fervent tongue-in-mouth dives make her feel wanted and appreciated. Like a woman. A feeling she has not experienced for a long time…maybe ever. Up to now she has been taken by rough boys who forced her to do for them what they would not do for her. Tonight she feels special. The friction in her loins that drives her toward bliss overcomes the discomfort of the tightening around her neck. The two opposite feelings from opposite parts of her body unite, equal in intensity. Gradually the pressure of choking becomes the dominant experience. She looks at him, and he is smiling. It is not a happy smile, but one of conquest. Sardonicus incarnate. She is frightened and reaches to her neck to pry loose his hands. They are locked and coming together tighter.

"Stop. Please stop."

"Not yet, sweet Annalee. You're not yet at the Promised Land. Soon, my dear, very soon."

His grip is like a vise. His thumbs press down on her throat. Her larynx is nearly shut altogether. No air. She starts to thrash. Her eyes are bugged out. She scratches his shoulders and tries to reach his face. He removes his right hand and lands a crushing blow in the middle of her forehead. Her eyes roll. She kicks uselessly. The cowboy will break the bronco, in life and in spirit. Her thrashing becomes twitches. There it is—the face, the look in the eyes. At the moment of death, the pinnacle of an orgasm, and at child birth, the look is the same. This moment is the perfect fusion of opposites: pain and pleasure—agony and ecstasy. Then stillness. Over the past twenty years, the little man has seen this face before. Street walkers, bar pick-ups, young runaways, and wayward wives. He seeks the look. It is his reward.

"I'd ask you how you liked it, but I can already see that it was drop dead great for you. By the way, I came again just as you died. So, you could say it was great for me, too."

He withdraws and lies beside his silent amore notti. He must rest for a few minutes before he disposes of the body.

He dresses her and then himself. He walks to the back of the saloon. There is a black pick-up truck, a white four-door Oldsmobile, and the girl's blue Malibu. He gets in, starts the engine, revs it so that anyone in the bar will hear it, and drives to the motel. There he loads her body into the passenger seat and heads up the foothills on a two-lane country road. About two miles on the journey, he comes to a sharp curve. He stops, backs up, and slides Annalee's body over to the driver's side on top of him. About fifty feet from the curve and the rusty guard rail, he extricates himself from beneath her. As he opens the driver side door, he steps on the accelerator. The car roars toward the guard rail, and he tumbles out just before the rail. The car lurches through the railing, pausing momentarily, and then plummets to the ravine below. The crash echoes. He dusts himself off and walks deliberately back to his motel room. A pleasant evening was had by all. Or at least by Mr. Benjamin Dover.

Chapter 12

The vibrating buzz of his cell phone on the bedside table awakens the little man.

"Hello."

"Are you at the motel?"

"Yes"

"We'll come and pick you up in two hours."

"Okay."

The motion of the plan is accelerating. He must search the room to be sure there is no trace of his late night visitor. Then a change of clothes back into his traveling suit, a fresh shirt, and tie. He is about to visit a client and must look serious. Two hours, 120 minutes, 7,200 seconds. Anxiety builds as time is parsed and moves so slowly.

The forceful knock on the door to the man's room startles him.

"Ready, counselor?"

"Yes."

"Let's go and meet the rest of the team."

The silver-gray SUV heads east into the flatland. About thirty-minutes into the journey, there appears a truck stop. The sign reads *Food. Fuel. Showers*. The little man spots another silver-gray SUV beside an army hummer and a blue eighteen-wheeler. A few men are milling around the vehicles. He approaches a large scruffy white man.

"What are we waiting for?"

"The rest of the men to shower and eat, but more important we're waiting for our native guide. So just relax. When he gets here, we roll. From now on, there is no turning back. We ride for power and glory."

How quaint, the little man thinks.

The caravan is ready and fully loaded—one DOC Land Rover with Eliot Livingston and Office Robert Jones, one army hummer with five large white men, and two silver-gray SUVs with two large white men and two boney black men each. The blue over land carrier sits empty at the truck stop. This vehicle blends in with the others.

The caravan heads out to the federal correctional facility in silence. Everyone knows his duties and responsibilities. About a mile from the facility, the caravan stops. The Hummer and the two SUVs seek cover behind some sage brush on the sides of the road. Then the Land Rover proceeds to the desired destination. The men in the hidden vehicles double-check their weapons. They are ready. Sweat from the heat of the rising sun and anxiety covers all of them. They await the signal.

Eliot begins to feel the manifestation of being anxious. "Office Jones, are you ready to do what you must do to reap the fantastic reward that awaits us all? Are you positive the scanners won't detect my special gifts?"

"I've done my time in this hell hole. So, yes I'm ready. And, yes, you and your gifts will pass through with ease. Now get out your ID for the gate guards."

The two men and the Land Rover separate from the

others. The entry process is seamless. The Land Rover is backed into its parking space for easy exit. All other vehicles are parked front against the wall. The two men enter the large solid door and walk purposefully down the hall toward the office of Warden Jenkins. They pass through two metal detectors without causing a disturbance.

"Good day, Mr. Livingston. We're ready for your visit. Katherine Samuels will be delivered to the conference room at your say so."

"Thank you, Warden. Before I meet with my client, I must go to the bathroom, if you don't mind."

"Yes, sir. There's one off the conference room. Please use that. That'll be all, Office Jones, thank you."

Once inside the bathroom, Eliot sits and discharges the lubricated condom. He fishes it from the bowl, unties it, and removes fourteen nine-millimeter hollow-point cartridges that are hot loaded. These are known as cop killers, because they can pierce armor and wreak lethal damage on the policeman wearing the vest. He loads the plastic gun, washes his hands, and flushes the commode. The loaded gun is safely hidden.

"Warden, I'm ready to meet my client."

The door opposite the lawyer opens and two guards usher the client into the small room. She shuffles up to the chair opposite her lawyer. The shackles at her feet rattle. She keeps her hands at her side. She has to. They are secured by cuffs attached to a waist chain. The guards forcibly put her into the chair. Her hand cuffs are attached to the metal arms of the chair. The leg shackles are attached to the front legs of the chair. There is no expression from anyone in the room.

"When you're done, please knock on the door. We'll come and fetch her."

"That will be all. Thank you."

The solid metal door is slammed closed so that the two remaining in the room know who is the boss. Eliot opens his attaché case and removes two manila files. He knows that no one outside the room is observing his actions. He also knows that the room is bugged. So he speaks in legal banalities as he sets in motion the planned escape by pressing speed dial number one on his cell phone. No need to speak, because the signal does that for him. He knows that in exactly ten minutes those on the inside must act, because in exactly ten minutes those on the outside will act. It is ten thirty-four a.m. on Wednesday.

He opens one folder and slides it over the table to his client. "I think we're beginning to create a good case for appeal. You'll note on page two some new favorable facts have come to light."

On page two is the cuff key supplied by Officer Jones.

Ms. Samuels slowly and carefully reaches for the key with her left hand and unlocks the cuff on her right wrist. The she repeats the process for her left hand and both legs. The chains and shackles are undone, but do not fall on the floor as Eliot continues to ramble about recommendations from people in high places, unfavorable witnesses unavailable, etc. etc., ad nauseum. He is speaking for the recording devices so he speaks loudly about nothing. He glances at his watch and withdraws the loaded plastic nine-millimeter hand gun. It is ten twenty-nine a.m.

 espeso

The hummer and the two SUVs are sprinting toward the compound gate. Then suddenly they screech to a halt about 100 yards from the entrance. Two large men get out of the Hummer. Each has an RPG on his shoulder. All the white men exit the SUVs. Each has an assault weapon of some kind. It is now ten thirty-two a.m. The fireworks are about to commence.

"*Now!*"

The RPGs let loose their payload and are reloaded. As the front gate explodes the RPGs are fired at the main entrance to the prison. It, too, explodes into wreckage. A complete opening, like a tunnel to freedom, is created. The assault weapons chatter destruction at the guards towers of the front gate. There is no return fire. The only noise is a claxon announcing an emergency at the prison.

෧෧෧

Fifteen seconds after the sound of the claxon, the door to the conference room bursts open and two guards appear. Eliot is waiting at the doorway. He puts two shots into the head of each guard. Ms. Samuels leaps from her seat. She sees Eliot smiling a delicious smile of evil accomplishment. The attorney lives to kill.

"Now give me the gun. It's time for you to play the hostage."

She stands behind him with the gun to his head and her arm around his neck as they step over the two bodies and out the door.

This is for show and not for go. They quickly walk down the hall. At the first of three hallway gates, they are greeted by Officer Jones who is holding Warden Jenkins from behind with a gun in his ribs.

"I got all the gates, Katherine. We can run straight to the getaway cars."

The escapees and hostages exit through the freedom tunnel to the main entrance.

෧෧෧

The large white men from the hummer turn when they hear the thump, thump, thump of the helicopters. Looking away from the prison, they see two choppers above them creating a swirling mass of dusty air. One is a gun ship and the other a personnel carrier. There is also a dust cloud of federal vehicles about a quarter mile away. The men turn and commence firing at the helicopters as they near. Fire is returned from the M-134D Gatling Gun mounted on the side of one chopper. With its 3,000 round per minute firing rate, the M-134D simply sprays the Archangels with metal death. In less than ninety seconds the area where the Archangels stood is turned into a mass of body parts on a bloody bog of sandy soil. They never had a chance. The black garbed men exiting the personnel carrier disperse and take up firing positions.

The guard tower comes alive with four men. They had been in hiding as if they knew what would happen. There is no reason for them to fire, because there was are no invaders to kill. The M-134D is turned on the Hummer and one SUV. Within a minute the vehicles are jagged heaps of useless metal. The vehicles' windows are missing and tires are flat. Each engine compartment is substantially perforated. Flames burst from the fuel tanks. The federal vehicles arrive in time to start the crime scene clean up and information gathering.

঎঎঎

In the opening that once was the prison's main entrance stand Officer Jones and Katherine Elizabeth Samuels with their hostages. They are recognized by the federal clean-up crew. A bull horn blares out, "Halt. Stay where you are. Don't move, or you'll be shot."

"We have hostages. If you shoot at us, they'll die."

"Ms. Samuels. Officer Jones. Put down your weapons and release the hostages. This can end peaceably."

As expected Ms. Samuels speaks for the pair. "No. That's not the way it's going to go down. We have plans. Here's what you'll do. You'll take us, my compatriots and our hostages, out of here to a place of our choosing. When we get to that place, we'll free the hostages and be on our way. You have three minutes to decide if the hostages live or die."

The federal agents can deal with the hostage takers, but have no idea who the compatriots are. They failed to notice the silver-gray SUV that escaped to the east, prior to all the explosions and gun fire.

"Give us a little more time. We need to get the transportation ready."

Ever so slowly, the two snipers get Jones and Samuels in their crosshairs. They both announce to their commander, "Target acquired."

Snipers hidden in the tall grass await the authorization to take down their targets. It comes in ten seconds.

"You have a green light."

Whup! Whup! Jones and Samuels are pushed back from their hostages by the impact of the .762 caliber slugs. Their heads explode and disappear in a red mist of blood and brain matter. Officer Jones's service Glock and the plastic gun held by Ms. Samuels are tossed aside by the impact.

Warden Jenkins and Eliot Livingston have blood on them, but they are free. The federal agents rush to them.

"Thank god you saved us. I thought we'd be dead for sure."

"Mr. Livingston, you're under arrest for facilitating the attempted prison escape of Katherine Elizabeth Samuels, murder, attempted murder, obstruction of justice, and other charges too numerous to recount."

"What the hell do you mean? I was a hostage. My life was in danger."

"Cut the act, counselor. You've been under surveillance for months. We knew what you were going to do. We just didn't know how or when. We know you secreted a specially made handgun into the prison with the assistance of Officer Jones. We assumed that you gave that gun to Ms. Samuels, who used you as a phony shield. It was your plan all along to get her out of prison. The two of you had plans to escape to Africa with the money you and your pals had accumulated. So, shut the fuck up and turn around to be cuffed."

At that moment, Eliot drops to the ground and grabs the plastic gun. As his hand wraps around the piece, he is hit by four shots from the federal .45 caliber hands guns. He crumples and dies in the dust.

The prison has been in lock down. Now, the crime scene is locked down. The technicians gather all the pertinent facts, data, and evidence. The prison's construction crew will rebuild the gate and entrance. The ground will be plowed and seeded. No reporters have been or will be called. Total radio silence. In two weeks, no one will suspect that the firefight and deaths occurred. Now you see it, now you don't. That's the way the federal government wants this mess to end and not be remembered.

☙❧

The silver-gray SUV bounces on the country road until it reaches a four-lane highway and roars toward freedom. The four boney black men inside the SUV are giddy when they discover the cash that the little man was going to use to pay for the flights. They have $400,000 of found money and a highly functional vehicle to get them to New York. They were about to complete the vendetta. Someone had to pay for their lost future.

❧❧❧

The clamor of the evening meal is interrupted by Tony.

"Okay, guys. Listen up. I'll be traveling on business the first part of next week. I leave on Sunday evening and return Wednesday evening. When I have returned from previous trips, your mother has informed me that you three have not been on your best behavior. Your mother and I recognize that part of your disruptive behavior stems from the fact that you miss me. I'm flattered. But the biggest driving force of your behavior in my absence is that you're testing your mother. You scream, because you can, because she's too gentile and too loving to tell you the shut the hell up and behave. That's disrespectful of her and because I love her, you behavior is disrespectful of me. And that hurts her and me.

"So, here's the deal. During the three days of my absence, you'll treat your mother and each other with respect and love. Just as you treat me. Leave your high energy levels and rowdiness at school. I really don't want to come home and find out that you have been disrespectful of your mother because you thought you could get away with it behind my back. That will never happen. Got it."

"Yes, Dad."

"Yes."

"Yes."

"Dad, where are you going this time?"

"Cassandra, I'm going to Baltimore, Lancaster, Pennsylvania, and Philadelphia."

"What kind of crime wave could the Amish cause?"

"Not sure. But, because of their long history of isolation within the county at large due to their religious beliefs, the Amish keep the local police and sheriff offices at arm's length. And, consequently the police departments have been reluctant to rush in and solve crimes such as extortion, gambling, and robbery. But recently, there have been two murders, which police think might be related to those crimes. The Lancaster County Sheriff's office has requested my presence to help them better understand how to properly investigate major crimes, such as murder. And, perhaps walk back the investigation to the other lesser crimes."

"Dad?"

"Antonio."

"It sound like they don't know what they want, but they'll know it when you tell them."

"Yes, it does, sort of. Now, the three of you, off to bed."

"My dear husband. How can I ever repay you?"

"I'll take care of dinner clean up, while you put your thinking cap on and try to conjure a method of showing your deep, heartfelt appreciation for my stand with the three demons. Now, leave me alone in the kitchen."

Melissa's grin is flirtatious.

✑✑✑

Sunday arrives with all the rush of reading the paper. Sections strewn upon the solarium floor. Coffee cup on the table. The remains of a bialy and lox are dwarfed by the serving plate. Both adults are still in their sleeping attire at ten-thirty a.m.

"Melissa, how about we go to the park for a stroll and picnic?"

"That sounds great, but how are you going to tear the children away from their video games?"

"As lord of the manor, I'll demand it."

"Good luck with that."

"Watch and learn, fair maiden. Hey, guys, Waddaya say to a picnic in the park?"

The silence of denial was ear shattering. Tony walks into the hall and repeats his question—this time at several decibels higher. Silence. He knocks on the door to the boy's room. Silence. He enters cautiously. There are his two male beasties engrossed in some war like game. The point of view with the soldier looking down the barrel of an oddly shaped large automatic weapon. He is being shot at and he is killing bad guys. Both his boys have buds in their ears yet the sound of weaponry is so loud Tony can hear it from eight feet away. He reaches a lamp on one of the desks and turns it on-off-on-off-on-off to get their attention.

"How about the family has a picnic in the park to-day?"

"Sounds good. When do you want to go?"

"Twelve-thirty. That will give you guys time to finish this uncomfortable game and clean-up your room. Take the entire service for eight which seems to be scattered around this cave to the kitchen and put it all in the dishwasher. We'll stop at the deli on Ninety-First Street for sandwiches and stuff. It'll be fun."

Cassandra is standing outside her brothers' room. She heard everything. "My room is neat."

Her competitive nature is sometimes used to flirt with her father. This is one of those times.

"Okay, Cassandra, I put you in charge of collecting Frisbees and tennis balls. I will be in charge of the blankets and food."

Tony returns to the solarium.

"Did you succeed in your quest, oh lord of the manor?"

"All is in the works. Departure time is twelve-thirty. M'lady hath naught to do but enjoy."

୧୬୧

The early May weather is perfect. Sounds abound in the park. Music of nearly every Central and South American nation. Hundreds of families. After about thirty minutes of Frisbee and tennis toss they have deli lunch. A baseball game is being played on all the eight diamonds. Tony and Antonio stroll over the games. Antonio wants to watch the catchers. Some a good and some are older weekend warriors, whose dream past them twenty years ago. Half an hour is enough. On their way back to the family blanket, Tony takes no notice of the two sets of two very black boney faced men sitting in the shade beneath opposite trees about fifty yards from Melissa, Bartheleme, and Cassandra.

The happy and tired family heads for home. Tony will leave his loved ones for Baltimore at five p.m. for a seven-thirty flight. Adolfo will drive Tony to the LaGuardia.

<h1 style="text-align:center">Chapter 13</h1>

Good morning. I'm Antonio Sattill. I was a captain in the New York Police Department and was in charge of the Manhattan Crime Analysis team. During my watch we had the occasion to investigate and solve the Handyman Murders and the REACH Mission case, both of which made national headlines and solidified the need for and the procedures of CAT. But, since I'm retired and my elder son is named Antonio, please call me Tony. I appreciate the opportunity to come before you today to discuss those procedures and answer any questions you might have about them or any issue which are before you in Charm City. I'm not here to solve your murder cases or tell you what to do. I wish only to share my experience, in the hope that it offers you a fresh way look to at difficult situations. Again, thanks for inviting me."

Tony speaks for about a half an hour then opens the mic for questions. They start as mundane procedural issues, but after eight or so the questions turn to the three murders in the harbor area. Tony turns to slides of a hypothetical murder scene and provides further edification about his theory of investigative spheres. He notes several officers are taking notes and several are texting people outside of the seminar. After three hours, the seminar concludes. Tony begins to prepare his departure and the three-hour drive to Pennsylvania Dutch country. He is interrupted by a young woman.

"When are you leaving?"

"And you are?"

"Detective Mary Ann Buckwalter."

"Well, Detective Buckwalter, I'll leave as soon as I'm packed up and can visit your commander, thank him, and get directions out of the city. Why do you ask?"

"I just thought—nothing. Thanks for the insight. We desperately need a CAT squad. We seem to be tripping over the ME's feet with every murder. But, as you noted, the old line detectives—or as I like to call them, the defectives—love the status quo. They do the traditional investigation and get all the glory. They're slower than molasses in January. If we had CAT, the process would speed up and our close rate would increase. By the way, how do you explain that fact that your commanders let CAT run the complete investigation of the REACH Mission?"

"I attribute their decision to their willingness to let my team do all the heavy lifting and take all the risks. If we succeeded, the commanders would take the credit. We did and they did. Had we failed, they would have denied any involvement. We would have taken the big hit—a two week rip or maybe a demotion to walking the beat on Staten Island."

"I'm sorry you have to leave so soon. There's so much more I could learn from you."

"You have good people over you. Listen to what they tell you and ask of you. Decipher what action is truly needed and go full bore. That has always worked for me.

Now I really have to leave. I don't like to drive at night on unfamiliar roads. Thanks for attending the seminar."

Being hit on has not happened to Tony for about two decades. His ego was temporarily inflated. She was attractive, but a one-night stand would complicate his life way too much. And if Melissa ever found out about an indiscretion, she would fulfill her promise to "staple that thing to your thigh while you sleep."

His wife can be very motivating.

☙❧

Tony calls while he is heading north to Lancaster.

"Hey, sweetie, how has your day been?"

"Lonely, but the children have been a joy. By the way, after I ran the dishwasher, I emptied it and discovered plates and glasses I thought were long lost. The boys have to do a better job of policing their room on a regular basis. Thanks for getting the dear ones to clean up their cave. How was Baltimore?"

"As I had suspected. A good Q and A at the end of my talk. I think I made an impact on the department's commanders. CAT may find its way into the Baltimore PD within a few years. I'm now headed to Lancaster. I miss you sweetie."

"I miss you, too. Do you want to talk to the children?"

"No, I don't want them to think that I don't trust them to do what I request and that I'm checking up on them. I'm leaving I-Eighty and turning onto Route Thirty. Lancaster in twenty-eight miles. The Hilton is on the far side of the city. So I guess I have about thirty five miles to go before I sleep. I'll call tomorrow. Sleep well."

"You, too."

The last part of the trip is over roads under construction with blinking yellow lights and detours. Thirty-five miles takes an hour. Check in is a breeze. The bar is open. Two drinks and to bed.

୧୬୧

"Good morning. I'm Antonio Sattill. I was a captain in the New York Police Department and was in charge of the Manhattan Crime Analysis team. During my watch we had the occasion to investigate and solve the Handyman Murders and the REACH Mission case, both of which made national headlines and solidified the need for and the procedures of CAT. But, since I'm retired and my elder son is named Antonio, please call me Tony. I appreciate the opportunity to come before you today to discuss those procedures and answer any questions you might have about them or any issue which are before you in the Red Rose City. I'm not here to solve your murder cases or tell you what to do. I wish only to share my experience in the hope that it offers you a fresh way to look at difficult situations. Again, thanks for inviting me."

Tony speaks for about a half an hour then opens the mic for questions. They start as mundane procedural issues, but after eight or so the questions turn to the murders in the county. Tony turns to slides of a hypothetical murder scene and provides further edification about his theory of investigative spheres. He notes several officers are taking notes and several are texting people outside of the seminar. After three hours and much discussion, the seminar concludes. Tony begins to prepare his departure and the three-hour drive to the land of cheese steak sandwiches. He must have a late lunch with the sheriff, the cousin of Bill Davis, a long-time NYPD friend.

"Sheriff, I think I can appreciate how difficult it must be to investigate crimes among people who don't want you in their world. I can also appreciate how much pressure you must be feeling from the non-Amish population or the English as they call us. You're really caught in an awkward situation—damned if you do and damned if you don't."

"Tony, if you were in my position, what would you do?"

"I would never presuppose to tell you what to do."

"I'm asking you as one fellow law enforcement officer in a tight spot who seeks the assistance of another officer who has experienced tight spots on a far bigger scale. You see, I know about what you went through during your two big cases. Suspicion of guilt and lack of support from your bosses. The proverbial rock and hard place."

"Okay. No holds barred. I would have a very frank meeting with the church elders and tell them that you're about to put on a full-court press. You're going to dig, roust, and investigate everyone who has shit on his shoes. Tell them that your job is to clean up any messes so that the plain folk can live in peace and tourism can flourish. And if they have any objections to your plan, tell them to put them in writing, and you'll address them after your work is done. This approach will ruffle feathers, but remember, I'm a New Yorker. We tend to be so direct our actions appear to be rude. But we get the job done."

"Thanks. I'll take your personal counsel under advisement. Do you need any directions to Philadelphia?"

"Thanks, but no. I have the address and the car has a GPS. I better be on my way to avoid rush hour traffic on the Schuylkill Express Way. I understand it can be a royal pain."

As he gets to his car, Tony looks at his watch. Three-thirty p.m. Immediately upon starting the car, Tony's telephone rings. It is Melissa.

"Tony, they're gone. The children have been kidnapped—Adolfo was unable to pick up the children. There was something wrong with our car, and when he got to the school, the children had already been picked up. He learned that two tall, boney dark black men in chauffer's livery escorted my babies into their limo, and then they just drove off."

Melissa stopped screaming and paused for a breath.

"Melissa, if Adolfo is with you, put him on the line."

"Mr. Sattill, I'm really sorry. When I went to get the car to pick up the children, it would not start. When I lifted the hood, I saw that the battery cables had been cut. I knew this was a sign of big trouble. I called the school, but couldn't reach the teacher in charge of pick-up. I hailed a cab and went to the school. I was told that the two black guys had appeared dressed like limo drivers and told the school that I was ill. They said you had hired a service to take the children home. It all seemed legit to the teacher, so the school let the children go with the guys. A bit of good news is that one of the teachers remembered the license plate of the limo. I wrote it down. Now what?"

"Call Lieutenant Chris Wills and give him the number and tell him why he's getting it. He'll trace the number to the company. That's the start. Then tell him to be at my apartment at seven tonight. Then call Lieutenant Brendan McLaughlin and tell him what has happened and to meet at my apartment at seven tonight. Here are the two telephone numbers. After you have done this, stay with Missus Sattill. She'll need a rock. That's you, Adolfo."

"Will do, sir. Here's Missus Sattill."

"I'm petrified. I knew something bad was going to happen—but, no, super cop had it all under control. I was afraid my babies would become disposable pawns in your quest for glory. Now they're gone. What can we do?"

"Have you heard anything from the kidnappers?"

"No. Does that mean my children are dead?"

Her hysterical sobbing has stopped, her staccato conversation has slowed, and her breathing is beginning to sound normal.

"Since we have not heard from the kidnappers, it's reasonable to assume they're formulating their plan. They'll wait so we fret and stew. Then, when they think we're in a state of full-blown anxiety, they'll call with the ransom demand."

"I'll pay them whatever they want to get back my babies safe and sound."

"Let's not get ahead of ourselves. I'll be home by seven. Chris and Brendan will come over. Then we can establish courses of reaction to their demands. Don't talk to anyone about this. Ask Carmelita to stay until I get home so there are several people in the house. Adolfo will drive her home."

"It's your fault."

She slams the phone down. The silence stings like iodine in an open wound.

☙❧

Tony races to the Pennsylvania Turnpike toward New Jersey. He well exceeds the speed limit to get to the Garden State. He calls the New Jersey State police; reaches an old friend, Commander Simmons; and tells him he needs an escort and why it is necessary. Commander Simmons alerts the highway division. When Tony crosses over from the Pennsylvania Turnpike to the

New Jersey Turnpike, he is met by two patrol cars. The three speed off. Tony is behind his escort. Tony's rental car has never driven this fast this long. The three vehicle wagon train covers one hundred and ten miles in less than eighty minutes. He arrives at the Lincoln Tunnel.

Normal traffic flow into Manhattan. Then the tortuous drive to the Upper East Side. He roars across lower Manhattan and takes the East Side Drive north exiting at 72nd street.

Not much traffic—he caught a break. He screeches the car to a halt in front of his building. As the door man approaches to shoo him away from the treasured spot, he notices Tony and grabs his bag.

"They're waiting for you, sir."

"Who's waiting?"

"Your wife, driver, maid, two police lieutenants, and your in-laws. Geeze, I hope I didn't give away the surprise. Is it your birthday?"

"No, it's not my birthday. Thanks, anyway."

The elevator can't go fast enough. As he steps through the doors onto his foyer, he is met by Melissa. He reaches out to hug her, and she slaps him hard.

"Welcome home, oh lord of the manor and killer of children."

Her Ivy League cynicism fueled by anger drives her to violence.

"Melissa, that's enough. Come with me, where we can both calm down."

Melissa and her mother walk arm-in-arm into the solarium. Tony asks Adolfo to drive Carmelita home and return as quickly as possible. Then, he, Chris, Brendan, and Jerry go to the dining room table.

"Gentlemen, this will be the command post, because this is where the bad guys will call. All three of my children know the numbers for me and Melissa. And I'm sure, by now, the bastards have gotten that information. What have you two learned? Chris?"

"The limo belongs to A-One limo service. They acknowledge that they have lost the vehicle. The company has not yet put Lo-Jacks in the limos. They claim it is for cost control. Regardless, this particular limo had a pick-up on Van Wyk Avenue at noon. It never showed and the driver is not answering his cell phone. I issued a BOLO for the car to all boroughs and New Jersey."

"Brendan?"

"Going on the safe bet that the perps are our four Ethiopian felons, Benny Radle, David Ellis, Wilson Abraham, and Ernest Davis, I issued a BOLO with their mug shots. I noted that they were wanted in connection with the robbery of the Spartan Services armored truck. They're described as armed and extremely dangerous. The department is advised to observe and report to me, but not to approach."

"The key for us is to keep the truth of this event off the police radar and out of the news. Understood?"

"Tony, in my zeal to help, I may have erred. I called a few of my friends at One Police Plaza and told them of the event. They promised to back channel their efforts to keep it out of the media."

"Damn, Jerry. Sorry. The old cronies downtown will do anything to get their name in ink or their voice on the news. Public exposure is needed to justify their existence. Okay, we now know what we're up against. Chris and Brendan will advise all precinct captains, commanders, and information officers that all calls dealing with this event are to be routed to me. I will handle all calls for information."

"I'm sorry, Tony."

"It's okay, Jerry. Chris can you get me a techie, who can reprogram Melissa's phone so that all incoming calls roll over to my number. And I will need two department phones that carry no one's name. I will need to make calls when I receive calls."

"Tony, I'll have the techie here in fifteen minutes with three extra phones."

"Jerry, get back in touch with your pals and find out what they have learned and what they're doing. Remind them to be quiet. Three lives depend on their discretion."

"Tony, dear, Melissa would like to talk to you in private. Jerry, we must be leaving. Gentlemen, goodnight."

Almost in unison, "Goodnight, Missus Aylir. Goodnight, sir."

The elevator opens and closes twice and Tony's new team leaves.

As Tony walks toward the solarium, he hears the elevator opens for a third time.

"Sir, you wanted to see me?"

"Yes, I need you to do the family a huge favor. I want you to contact The Face and ask him if he would help me find my children. I know this is in violation of your parole, as was the gun you carried. I also know The Face has many feet on the street in Brooklyn. These feet have eyes, and they have friends in the other four boroughs. Ask him to just ask around."

"Sir, that's the least I can do. I owe you my new life, and I love your children. I would do anything to get the bastards who scooped them."

"Just ask The Face to ask around. That will be enough."

"Yes, sir. Goodnight"

Once again Tony heads for the solarium. The buzzing of the intercom interrupts his short trip.

"Mister Sattill, there's a police officer down here she says you asked for her."

"Yes, send her up."

As she steps off the elevator, she gawks in wonderment at the home of a retired police captain. She must be thinking, if this is what a pension buys, working twenty-five years on the force is worth it.

"Sir, you asked for me to program another phone to roll over all incoming calls to yours and for a few clean phones."

"Just a minute, Officer Tate. I'll get you the other phone. Here's mine. Melissa, dear, I need your phone."

"Why?"

"I'll explain in a few minutes. Officer Tate, here is the phone from which all incoming calls are to be re-routed. How long will this take?"

"Three minutes or less."

Time drags. She has completed her task. "Here you are, sir, and here are the clean phones. Will there be anything else?"

"No, and thank you very much. Goodnight."

"Goodnight."

The elevator is locked down. Tony enters the solarium. "Sorry, Melissa. Just a technical issue."

"What's with my phone?"

"Until this crap is over, all incoming calls on your line will be routed to my phone. One line of communication with the bad guys. I'll tell any friends of yours that we're suffering a technical melt down, and you'll call them back. Then you use this phone to call them back. It's a clean police phone."

"Okay, I understand. I want you to know that I'm sorry for slapping you and demeaning you in front of those people. That was childish. But I still blame you for what has happened to our babies. Notice I said 'our.' I understand that you were following your police instinct to solve crimes. But I also understand that you never thought your pursuit of justice would come to this. Now, tell me what your plan is?"

"I have no grand plan. I wish I did. We must wait to hear from the perps. Then we can act and react. Right now we're in the dark. Helpless and in the dark, forced to wait patiently. I know more tomorrow."

At this point, he notices the stubby of a drink in his wife's hand.

"I need a drink. Sweetie, can I refresh yours?"

"Yes, I need to sleep soundly."

Regardless of the hour, it has been a long day. They both fall asleep quickly.

The buzzing of Tony's phone causes him to stir and reach for the night table without opening his eyes.

"Hello."

"We have your spawn, and you and the black whore will pay dearly to get them back. Listen tomorrow for instructions."

"Wait—"

The man hangs up.

Now, Tony can't go back to sleep. A dozen scenarios clog his brain. Melissa does not awaken. His eyes do not close. Dawn is one hundred hours away.

Chapter 14

It's five forty-four a.m. Dawn is about to happen. Tony's phone rings again.

"Hello."

"Tony, this is Ray Martani. I learned you got big trouble dumped on your shoulders. And I'm here to help."

Ray Martani, a fellow NYPD stiff who got himself in a territorial jam at big shoot out. The feds had arrived at Ray's crime scene, at Nite Lites, an afterhours rave joint. They were in the process of stomping on the evidence and usurping command, when Tony showed up and resolved the issue.

"I'll never forget how you got my ass out of the fire and gave me some press creds. I told you then, I owed you. Now it's time to pay. What can I do?"

"Ray, where are you?"

"Right now, I'm on my way to work, which is in the Brooklyn Borough Chief's Office. My office."

"I got nothing yet. One threatening call last night with the message to be ready for more today."

"Are Chris and Brendan helping you?"

"Yes."

"Then you have the best support. Just to let you know if there is anything you need—even outside the box—let me know and it's yours."

"Thanks, pal. I can't tell you how much that means. There is one thing."

"Name it."

"I put feelers out to the Colucci family to ask around. If you could, keep an eye on the family foot soldiers. They might get aggressive and, wishing to curry favor, do something stupid. That would be a big relief."

"Considerate done. By the way, we got the two BO-LOs and I will stress today that these are top priority. I will demand a report at the end of each shift as to geography covered, et cetera. I'll stay in touch."

"Thanks, Ray. By the way—"

"No, I dress like a borough chief now. I keep the Hawaiian shirts and silver forty-fives at home on Long Island. My wife and kids won't even let me take them out of the closet for Halloween."

Well, the word is on the street. The intercom buzzes.

"Mister Sattill. There are three policemen down here to see you."

"That's okay. Send them up."

"Sir, we're all sorry to hear your plight. We'll keep good thoughts for the children."

"Thanks. Jesus, you guys are early. Did you sleep at all?"

"We did. How about you?"

Tony tells them about the telephone call.

"We figured the bastards would call late at night just to keep you and Missus Sattill on edge. That's why we brought this equipment. You remember Officer Tate. She will hook up the equipment so we can trace any calls."

"Yes. Good morning, Officer Tate."

"Tony, what's all the commotion? What is all this electronic equipment? Sorry, good morning to all of you. I'm Missus Sattill, but since I suspect we'll be in close quarters for a period of time, please call me Melissa. I know Chris and Brendan. Who are you?"

"My name's Jenny Tate. I'm the technician assigned to Lieutenant Wills's precinct. I'm responsible for setting up the telephone tracking device that monitors all incoming calls. I'm sorry that we had to meet under these circumstances, ma'am."

"Melissa, please, Jenny."

"If you'll excuse me, I have a lot of work to do."

"I have coffee to make, and, for me, aspirin to take. Can I get any of you any breakfast?"

"Not for me, thanks. Coffee would be great." In unison.

☙❧☙

Ten-thirty a.m. Tony's phone buzzes. Everyone is silent. Five rings is enough time for Jenny Tate to get the tracking process started. Tony stares at his phone. The incoming number reads 212-599-3489.

"Hello."

"Good morning, Antonio Sattill, Captain NYPD retired. Did you sleep well?"

The voice is electronically altered.

"Who is this?"

"You know, but you don't know."

"What do you want?"

"We want you to suffer. As we have suffered. We want your wife, the black whore, to suffer as only a mother can suffer. We want five million dollars in unmarked bills by tomorrow noon. Delivery place to be determined."

"It will take me much longer than twenty-four hours to raise the money. I need three days."

"One day."

"Before you get any money from me, I need proof that all three of our children are alive and unharmed."

"I want to talk to the children," Melissa screams. "*Now!*"

"Oh, black whore, were you listening in? Are you upset? That's a shame. Maybe you can talk to your spawn later today. Maybe not."

Silence.

"What did you get?"

"Strange."

"That's not a word I want to hear. What was strange?"

"Did you hear the back ground noise? Traffic. And the call started on West Eighty-Eighth but ended on West Ninety-Eighth. It was truly a mobile call. My guess is that this guy was in a car with the windows down or on bicycle. I got the number, but if the caller was mobile, he probably tossed the burner down a sewer drain right after he hung up."

"How did he disguise his voice if he was on a bicycle talking on a burner?"

"We have this capability, but the civilian population does not. He must be very tech savvy. The kind of tech savvy one might learn in prison. He just applied his learned technology to communications."

"How do you come to that conclusion?"

"Mister Sattill, if I were in the shoes of the perp, I would make it nearly impossible for someone like me to trace calls. If we send patrols cars to check the sewer drains on the north bound side of all the West Side avenues from Ninety-Eighth Street to One Hundredth Street, my guess is that we'll find the burner phone, and it'll have finger prints on it. Or at least partials."

"Call me Tony. Thanks for the insight. I'm really glad you're here. Chris, can you get your precinct guys to do that immediately."

"Done."

"Folks. Carmelita has prepared Cuban sandwiches for lunch."

Halfway through his sandwich, Tony's phone buzzes. He lets it go for six rings.

"Hello."

"Tony, this is Ray Martani. I think we have something really big. We found the limo. Abandoned as expected. On Stuyvesant Avenue. But here's the best part. The car was spotted because it was parked with two wheels on the curb. While that's not unusual for Brooklyn, what *is* unusual is that the limo replaced a dark green van that had been parked in the same illegal manner. Several shop keepers had called in the van, and Traffic was set to tow it. So we have the license plate number, and we're tracing it now. I should have definitive information about the van and its owner within the hour. I'll call you then."

"Ray, I can't thank you enough."

"It's not over yet, Tony. But soon, baby, soon."

The intercom buzzes. "Mister Sattill, there are a bunch of reporters down on the sidewalk. They all want to talk to you and the missus."

"*No!*"

"That's what I told them, but they won't go away."

"Thanks. I'll take care of it."

"Carmelita and Adolfo will have to stay here until we can shoo away the blood suckers."

"Sir, if I may, I have a way to get rid of the unwanted. Let me make a call."

ঌঙঌ

The pattern for the day is established—periods of boredom and anxiety, separated by momentary bursts of frenetic activity.

"Tony, may I use one of the phones?"

"Sure, why?'

"I want to call the bank to be sure we have enough cash when it's needed."

Although Tony loathes the idea of paying a ransom, and he hopes it does not come down to that, he knows Melissa must do something to feel part of the team retrieving her children. The intercom buzzes.

"Mister Sattill, the reporters are going away. Now there are several large men on the sidewalk sort of keeping watch over the building. I don't know what happened, but we're back to almost normal."

"Thanks for the heads up." Tony turns to Adolfo. "Adolfo, I don't want to know what just happened, but thank you."

"I did nothing. No one is going to keep me prisoner. I like my freedom to come and go as I please. I'll take Carmelita home when she's ready. Do you want me to come back here or to stand by at my place."

"Stand by at home. I'll let you know when we need you. Thanks for all your help."

"It's the least I could do for you and Missus Sattill."

Chris's phone rings.

"Yes. Great. Check all of them against the prints of the four guys on the BOLO. Thanks. The sewer patrol came up with three cell phones. Lots of partials and smudges. They're cross matching to the prints of the four Ethiopians. We'll have an answer soon."

Tony's phone buzzes five times.

"Hello."

"Tony, this is Ray. We found the guy who owns the plates, but he does not own the van. He claims it was stolen yesterday. I'm afraid the car angle is a dead end. But we'll keep the pressure on. We're now canvassing the area to see if any of the citizens remember the occupants of the van. Hang tough, buddy."

"Thanks for your help."

The boredom part of the cycle returns.

Tony's phone buzzes five times.

"Hello."

"Good afternoon retired captain. How are you enduring the pain of anticipated loss?"

Tony signals to Jenny Tate. She has already started the tracking procedure.

"Is this Benny Radle, David Ellis, Wilson Abraham or Ernest Davis? Which one of you was riding the bicycle during the last call?"

Silence.

"You're not only arrogant, you're impudent and impotent. I suggest you do not try to trace this call while I hold a knife to the throat of your delicious daughter, Cassandra."

"If what you say is true, you're not on a bicycle. Maybe you're roaming the city in the dark green van with a stolen license plate."

Silence.

"Put Cassandra on the phone."

"Hello?" Cassandra sobs.

"Cassandra. This is Daddy. Are you all right? Have they hurt you, sweetie?"

"Daddy, come and get us. I'm scared."

Tony and the rest of the people in the room hear the sobbing.

"Let me talk to the boys."

"No. Have you gathered the money we requested?"

"Not yet. We need a few days to get that much cash."

"Tomorrow at noon."

"No. The day after tomorrow at five."

"Your arrogance will be the death of your children."

"When you call again, I want to speak to all three children. We want our children back in a safe and sound condition, and you want five million dollars. If we don't get our children back safely, you do not get the money. If you don't get the money, we won't get our children back. Look at this as strictly a business arrangement. It takes time to get five million. We have to sell stocks, and that takes three days to close.

"We have already started the wheels in motion to get the money, but the soonest we can get it is after four the day after tomorrow. That's the deal. If you harm our children or we don't get them back, you get nothing except the total wrath of the NYPD and the good citizens of New York. I'll have them all hound you to death. That's the deal."

"Where do you get the right to dictate terms to me?"

The caller is deep into rage as he sputters and spits out his words. Tony must remain calm and in control.

"Maybe we'll call this evening. Maybe we won't. Maybe it'll end this evening with the death of your children. Just stay by the phone."

Tony asks Office Tate, "Waddaya got?

"The call came from Queens in a roaming vehicle. I can isolate the area and we can send patrolmen to search for burner phones if you want."

Tony shakes his head. "Not necessary. We know who they are, or we'll confirm who they are by the prints on the first burner. I guess we better make sleeping accommodations for the three of you. Melissa honey, we need clean sheets for the beds in the children's rooms."

"Carmelita took care of that before she left."

By the evening, all are exhausted by the day's stress. Sweat stains are beginning to appear. Foreheads need to be wiped.

Chris's phone rings.

"You did. Great, thanks. The lad matched prints on one of the disposable phones to Benny Radle. So, their involvement is a lock."

"Thanks, Chris."

Tony's phone buzzes five times.

"Hello."

"Captain Sattill, this is Mason Roberts, of the *Ledger*. I would like to get some information from you about the kidnapping of your children."

"How the hell did you get this number?"

"That's not important. When were your children taken? Have you heard from the abductor or abductors? What demands have been made?"

"Slow down, Mister Roberts. I will not answer your questions over the phone. We should meet. Name the time and place."

"Margo Deli on East Ninety-Sixth Street in twenty minutes. See you then."

"Tony, what the hell are you doing? This was supposed to be kept quiet."

"Melissa, I have a plan. I'll be back in less than an hour."

❧❦❧

Margo deli is like many food establishments in the city. Small, crowded, noisy and smelling like good eating. Tony waits for three minutes before entering. This allows his three new friends to enter and sit near Mason Roberts.

When Tony enters the deli, he notices that Mason Roberts and Tony's three friends are the only people in the place. The staff appears to be in the back.

"Good evening, Mister Roberts. I'm Tony Sattill."

"Good evening, Mister Sattill. Here are my press credentials. I would like to ask you a few questions about the kidnapping of your children. I'll be recording our conversation for accuracy."

"No you won't, because there will be no conversation. No Q and no A. You're going to get up from this table and leave. And you'll leave me and my family alone."

"The kidnapping of a former police captain's children and the grandchildren of the former president of the city council is news, and the public has a right to know the news."

"That's where you're wrong. This is a personal situation, and I must insist that it be kept out of the public's eye."

"Are the kidnappers the same people you put in jail?"

"Goodnight, Mister Roberts."

"Are they demanding ransom? Your wife's fortune should be sufficient to cover any ransom demands."

"Goodnight."

Tony stands and nods to his three friends. As he leaves, he hears a commotion at the table and several chairs toppled. He turns to look. Two of the friends have clasped Mason Roberts's arms, while the third frisks him. His squirming is futile. The third man then delivers a hard punch to Mason's solar plexus. He crumbles gasping for breath. The cry for help will have to wait.

Halfway home, the three men catch up with Tony and hand him a large food bag containing a tape recorder, a body mic and recorder, a cell phone, and a note pad. The meeting never happened.

"Goodnight, Mister Sattill. We'll be here for the duration."

"Thank you. Goodnight."

Chapter 15

The intercom buzzes Tony awake. It's five twenty-six a.m.

"Mr. Sattill a guy just dropped off a package for you and the missus."

"I'll be right down, thanks."

The small box is wrapped in plain brown paper. The word, "Sattill" is scrawled on one side. The reverse side is taped. The box weighs next to nothing yet something moves back and forth as Tony gently shakes the package. The elevator to his foyer opens, and Tony is met by his team, sans Melissa.

"Let's open this in the kitchen on the big table. I'm sure this is not a bomb, but other than that, I have no idea what's inside. I want the paper checked for prints. The door men in the building wear white gloves, so any prints will be the delivery man's."

Tony judiciously cuts the tape and unfolds the paper surrounding the box. He hands the paper to Chris, who is calling his precinct for a messenger to pick up the paper and run it for prints. The box is approximately four inches by four inches. Plain white. Purchasable in any drug store or card shop. No clues to follow. Tony delicately removes the top and sees the message. His heart sinks.

Wrapped in tissue or toilet paper is the bloody finger of a child. He guesses it's the pinky.

"What's going on in here? Who's making coffee?"

"Sweetie, I'm not sure you want to be here now. We can discuss this later."

"What's in the box? I want to see."

Her scream is nearly ear shattering. She instantly turns to walk away, but spins around to more closely inspect the mutilated appendage. Between sobs she determines the rightful former owner.

"That's Antonio's finger. See how he bites his nails? I have nagged him repeatedly to stop that nervous habit, but to no avail. The bastards cut off his finger. Why?"

"Sweetheart, they want to show us how serious they are about getting the money."

"Well, give them the damned money today like they demanded. Shit, it's my money and they're my babies."

"It's not as easy as that. As long as we have the money, they're not going away. This gives us more time to find them."

"More time for them to mutilate our children— maybe kill one or two. Jesusfuckingchrist, you and the Ethiopians are like drunks at a fraternity fight. Neither of you is willing to bend until the other does. No compromise. They mutilate Antonio, you threaten them with a payment on your schedule. Well after their due date. *Reductio ad absurdum* dictates that after all our children are killed, you still won't give the kidnappers the money. So you'll claim victory. Well, if you remember correctly, that money is mine to with as I please. And I please to get my children returned without further damage done to them. When the bank opens, I'll get the five million, you'll set the meeting time and place, and I'll deliver the money and return with my children. So fuck you and your macho code."

"Melissa, think about what you're saying. The perps will, no doubt, want to see the money before they return our children. The perps know that all three children have seen them and can identify them when they're caught, and they *will* be caught. So, it's in the perps' best interest to leave no one behind who can finger them for this major crime—capital, if you consider that these guys are parolees. So their MO would be to take the money from you and tell you where they stashed the children, who are already dead. No, Melissa, the only leverage we have is the delay in delivering the money."

"Fuck you. Give me the finger. I want to preserve it with ice and salt water. Maybe it can be re-attached—if we get the children back in time."

Tony's cell phone starts to buzz. Jenny leaps into action, Brendan starts to dial his phone, and Chris is on the line with his precinct. After seven rings, Tony answers.

"Hello."

"Ah yes, retired Captain Sattill and the black whore, I hope your day has started pleasantly. By the way, your son is very brave, but he does not understand why he has to endure such great pain because of your arrogance and impudence."

"I see that you have reached the lowest level of desperation. Mutilation of a victim. In this case, a child. How brave you must feel. How cowardly you are. Harming our children cannot speed up delivery of the five million. The New York Stock Exchange has that part of the bargain within their control. And their rules are their rules."

"Since you and your bank know the money is coming, why won't they give you a very short term loan to protect the children from further damage? That seems simple enough."

"It doesn't work like that. Banks have their inflexible rules. We're both victims of those rules. Do not make the children victims, too. Harming children doesn't win you any popularity contests with the NYPD and the citizens of New York."

"I hope your black whore is listening. As the mother, she knows the value of her spawn. She'll do anything to protect them and keep them safe. Is that not correct, Missus Sattill?"

"Fuck you and your Ethiopian brothers. Leave my children alone, or I'll personally find you and cause you such incredible pain, you beg me for death, which will not come for a long time."

This is the mother tiger side—a side Tony has never seen.

"Such an idle threat from one so powerless. You're so brave hiding in your penthouse above the rest of the world."

"Who are you to talk about bravery? You hide behind little children. My husband is correct. You and the other jackals are cowards. Craven cowards. We'll have the money for you tomorrow after four p.m."

"It must be delivered today by noon."

"Impossible. Tomorrow after four."

"We'll see how strong your resolve."

Silence.

"I got him. East side going uptown between Eighty-Sixth and Ninety-Sixth."

"Captain, I sent sector cars to the intersections of the uptown avenues up to One Hundred Tenth Street. They're looking for a black man on a city racing bike. We'll get him."

❦

Traffic is a hump. Uptown, downtown, cross town.

Private cars, limos, taxis and busses clog the street and avenues. Pedestrians and cyclists clog the sidewalks and cross walks. At each intersection, there is a squad car checking the cyclists.

"This is car One-Four-Two to central. I'm at the corner of Third Avenue and Ninety-Eighth Street. I got him. He just blew through the intersection heading north. Black male, yellow and green racing jersey and green racing pants, but no helmet. He's hauling ass. I'm in pursuit. Central, alert other cars northbound."

"This is car One-Seven-Eight to Central. I'm pulling into the intersection of One Hundred Second Street and Third Avenue. I'm stopping all uptown traffic to allow One Hundred Second to clear heading west."

"Central, this is car One-Five-Nine. I'm pulling out onto Third Avenue from One Hundred Street."

"Central, this is car Two-Four-Seven. I'm heading south on Third Avenue from One Hundred Third Street. We have the suspect in a box."

Patrolman Sullivan and Gaynor leap out of the squad cars and approach the cyclist to apprehend him. Suddenly, the cyclist breaks through the traffic jam, swerves around cars, dodges pedestrians, and heads north. In his frenetic effort to escape the approaching officers, the black man does not see squad car 247.

BANG!

Man and bicycle hit the front of the squad car and are catapulted over the vehicle.

CRASH!

Man and bicycle land in a twisted heap behind the squad car, which screeches to a stop. Patrolman Jablonski leaps from the car and joins the two pursuing officers. No need to hurry, the cyclist is not going anywhere rapidly.

"I will call for a bus and back up, if you two will separate man from machine. Central we need a bus and additional man power for crowd control."

The cyclist's right leg is bent forward. Not the direction of a healthy knee. His arm is almost behind him. Not much visible blood. His moaning and gasping for air are labored as a result of the handle bar impaled in his stomach.

The crowd begins to form and come close to the squad car and cyclist. Sirens indicate the arrival of help. The man is given a cursory examination by the EMTs and lifted gently onto the gurney and into the ambulance. The ride to NYU General takes fifteen minutes.

ೞೞೞ

The hospital room is guarded by a young female officer. Chris and Brendan have been given permission to see the patient. Active police only. The bed looks like a strange marionette. Tubes are running from different places to various points of Benny Radle. The patient is cuffed to the side bars and his feet are shackled to the bed frame. It's too soon after the surgery to question him. The doctor listed the ailments—broken arm, fractured skull, dislocated knee, punctured abdomen, lacerated liver, and contusions over his body. Survival estimate is good if he can be left alone while his body and the medicines heal him. Maybe tomorrow he will be able to talk.

ೞೞೞ

The large room is set up like a dormitory. There are four bunk beds and three futons. Dirty towels are crammed into one corner of the room. The windows are high. No one can look in. There is a double door at one end of the room and a single door at the other. There appears to be a closet near the single door. Outside the closet are a sink, mini fridge, and a microwave on the counter. The floor is spotted with oil or grease stains.

Antonio sits on a lower bunk. Approximately two feet of heavy rope attach his right leg to the resting platform. He holds his hand, wrapped in a blood drenched towel, in front of him. Obviously in pain, but too brave to cry out loud, he moans occasionally. His face is ashen from trauma. A bowl of some type of food rests on the floor beside him.

Bartheleme appears to be resting on his bunk bed. Surreptitiously, he slides his hands down to his ankles and fumbles with the knots. He has been doing this for hours. The restraining loops have become slight looser. He thinks that in time he will be free. Not so sure what to do then. He has no plan.

Cassandra is prone on a futon resting on one elbow as she looks at her brothers. Every once in a while they relay winks or nods of communications. The large room is dark, except for light from the outside coming through the filthy windows. The men sit at a table twenty feet away.

"Little Cassandra. How pretty you are. Tell me, what do you do in school?"

"Work hard, and I'm participating in a science fair. I'll prove the Theory of Connectivity."

"How smart you must be."

"Yes."

"Have you ever been with a boy?"

"What do you mean 'been with'?"

"Have you had sex with a boy?"

"I'm twelve. I'm definitely not ready for sex."

"In my country, a twelve year old woman is of great value as a wife and mother. Much is given to the parents of a twelve year old bride by the family of her husband. Her purity is that valuable. If she's not pure, she's a whore and she'll not be married. When a woman is married, she becomes the possession of her husband. No man would pay for someone who is a whore. Whores have no value."

"That's sick."

"Your mother is a whore, because she was with your father when she was the possession of another. She violated her vows."

"That's none of your business. And, frankly, I doubt what you're saying. My mother and father love each other. And they love their children. That's all that matters."

"You're pretty. I'll wager there are many boys that would like to kiss you."

"I don't think so."

"Your skin is a beautiful shade of brown. Your eyes sparkle. And your figure is beginning to develop. I'm sure the boys have noticed you. Your curves. Or are they all blind?"

"I don't know."

"Well, I think you're pretty. Very pretty. And my friends think so, too. You would be a valuable bride in my country."

"Thank you. Now, when are we going to go home?"

"Soon. Right after your mother and father pay us for our pain and suffering."

"You're nothing more than petty criminals. First you take us. Then you ask for money. When my parents refuse to pay, you hurt Antonio. I need to get Antonio to a hospital. His cut will become infected. What's next?"

"You're as impudent as your father. Demanding when you have no right to demand is a very dangerous personality trait."

The boney black man is waved to the corner of the large room by the other boney black men. They whisper. Not softly. All are upset. They scream words in a foreign tongue. They gesture wildly. They turn toward the children and glare at them. The interrogator returns to Cassandra. The other two men head out the single door. Outside their screaming becomes louder. Their emotions run amok.

"Cassandra, dear, I think it's time you and I get to know each other better."

☙❧

Tony is frustrated by his inability to make good things happen. The elevator door opens and Adolfo appears.

"Adolfo, I thought we agreed you would stay at home and wait for my call."

"That was before I got a call from our friends in Brooklyn. They have some interesting news."

"Let's go to the solarium."

"First, Mr. Colucci sends his regards and prayers for the safe return of your children. He then tells me that one of his people noticed something interesting around the parked limo the police found on Stuyvesant Avenue. A few shop keepers and sidewalk generals noticed a couple of black guys getting out of the limo and into a dark green van. These sidewalk generals had seen the black guys before in the neighborhood. Buying food and booze. And weed from the street dealers. The black guys are tall and very thin—almost boney. Now the generals have not seen the black guys for the past a day or so.

"That part of Stuyvesant Avenue is all retail. Two blocks across the avenue from the bad parking job are apartments. Two blocks behind the avenue are warehouses. Abandoned and locked down almost as tight as Rikers Island. It's very possible that the kidnappers and the children are in one of the warehouses. Someone should check. Mr. Colucci hopes this information is helpful."

"Tell The Face that Missus Sattill and I thank him for this information. We'll pass it along to Captain Ray Martani, the Brooklyn Borough Chief. We'll wait two hours to allow anyone who should not be there to get out."

"Mr. Colucci told me the warehouses are empty of his people. So you can start to investigate immediately."

"Thanks, Adolfo."

Immediately, Tony calls Ray Martani and relays the information. Ray's on the case. He'll call as soon as possible with the results of the investigation.

Time drags forever.

ဢၧဢ

Chris and Brendan arrive, to the relief of Officer Tate. She wants to get fresh clothes. She came to the Sattills unprepared for an emotional siege. She has shown both lieutenants how to manipulate the technology on an emergency basis.

For a twenty-one-year-old rookie, this is an emergency. She leaves.

"Tony, we got nothing from our friend the bicyclist. He is so banged up he cannot talk and the doctors tell us to check back later today, after six."

Tony tells them about the lead to the whereabouts of the kidnappers.

They wait. Time drags.

ဢၧဢ

The boney black man loosens his belt and begins to lower his pants.

"What the hell do think you're doing?"

"As I said, we're going to get to know each other better."

"The hell we are."

By now Cassandra is yelling loudly. Bartheleme works feverishly on the knots. One leg is almost free.

"Look at my manhood. Soon it will be inside you. I will make you my twelve-year-old whore."

He reaches down to Cassandra's blouse and tears it open to reveal a camisole and a pre-teen chest just developing. He cups her breasts and smiles. She closes her eyes in fear. The man grabs her skirt and yanks it down to her ankles. Her light pink panties hide the fuzz that is the beginning of woman hood. Cassandra has yet to have her first period. Now her screaming reaches a fever pitch. She kicks and thrashes so that it is very difficult for the man to lie on her much less penetrate her. With one desperate move, she raises her knee with all her might. The knee finds the intended mark, and the man grimaces in pain, clutches his crotch and rolls off the futon. The pain is excruciating.

He pulls himself up onto the futon. Now he is angry. "Pain only makes the pleasure better. You will soon see."

The issue of readiness is now a problem for the man. Pain causes shrinkage and sometimes non-functionality. But he is persistent and takes his time. He yanks her panties down to the skirt at her ankles. His prize is in sight. He touches it and rubs it. His smile of conquest returns. His pants are off, and he is ready.

WONK!

Bartheleme has struck. He clings to the man's back as he pummels the back of his head with fists. The man screams, more startled than hurt. Bartheleme continues the barrage of punches. The man, naked from the waist down, struggles to toss his attacker off his back. The melee is frenetic, noisy, and brief.

"Let my sister alone, you bastard. Get off her, now."

The man rolls off the futon again, blinks, and rubs his head. Bartheleme remains on his back like on a piggyback ride. Except this rider is punching. The man's compatriots have to save him from the embarrassing onslaught of the child by pulling Bartheleme off and tossing him to the floor. Bartheleme slumps after being punched in the face. He does not stir. Blood trickles from his nose.

"You fucking bastards, you've killed him."

Antonio is no longer a bystander.

"Silence or you'll lose your whole hand."

Cassandra struggles to pull up her panties and skirt. She has more trouble with her camisole and blouse.

The three men gather in the corner to discuss their next move. Antonio is helpless. Cassandra cries. Bartheleme stirs slowly.

ↄ৵ↄ

"Tony, this is Ray. We searched warehouses in a ten by three block area from where the limo was parked. We got nothing. No doors pried open. Lots of broken windows. No one inside. I had my guys enter twenty-six buildings, and they found nothing but four-legged rats. Sorry, buddy."

"Thanks for your work, Ray."

Now Tony is up against a big ugly wall of time. He can't do squat until he hears from the kidnappers.

Chapter 16

Tony's phone rings five times.

"Hello."

"Good morning, Tony, this is Paul Tybor. I understand that you're in a very precarious situation."

"Yes."

"I also understand that you have been trying to handle the situation on your own. That is, without calling in favors from all your friends. Yes, you have tapped into the NYPD. Yes, you have even reached out to some less-than-upright characters. But you have access to friends like the Federal Kidnapping Unit of the FBI. If you would like the discrete assistance of this team of highly trained professionals, I can make that happen."

"God, Melissa and I would welcome any and all help we could get from your associates. But it must be immediate and kept off local media radar."

"I thought so. We can be there in thirty minutes."

"Thanks."

Tony outlines what additional help is on the way to Melissa then Chris, Brendan, and Jenny. Melissa hopes they will be swift and true. The others are stoic, adopting a wait-and-see attitude.

The intercom buzzes.

"Send them up."

Tony's telephone rings five times.

"Good Morning, Mister Sattill. This is Mason Roberts. We understand that you have sought the help of the FBI."

"Stop right there. Since they just arrived at my home, I can assume that you or one of your toadies is watching the door to my building. Most likely from across the street. Can you hold for a second?"

Tony buzzes the doorman and relays instruction for the men providing protection.

"Thanks so much for holding. By now, three men have surrounded the car from which you or your associate is spying on my life. Here's the deal. Back off. Drive away and the three men will not damage your vehicle and its occupant. If you drive away now and stay out of the way, I'm prepared to meet with you and give you all the details of this incredibly bizarre story. You'll have enough information to write a best seller. Maybe even receive a Pulitzer. Agreed?"

"How can I trust you to keep your word?"

"You can't. But then again, you can't risk having your vehicle and its occupant burst into flames either. So, Mr. Roberts, deal or no deal."

"Deal."

"You've chosen wisely. Now, go the fuck away."

Paul Tybor is standing in the foyer with two men dressed casually with FBI jackets. Each has a large duffle bag and a back pack.

"Thanks for coming, Paul. What do you plan to do?"

"First, let me introduce Special Agent Black and Special Agent White. They're electronics experts who have the latest in tracking equipment. Plus, they have been involved in hostage negotiations for a while. They're here to work with your people. Your people will still be the face of the situation. They'll lend their expertise to expand the capabilities of your team. Okay?"

"Agents Black and White, these are the team from the NYPD—Chris Wills, Brendan McLaughlin, and Jenny Tate. She's the tech wizard."

Handshakes all around. Faint smiles of friendship. They five settle in for a briefing.

"Tony, is there somewhere we can talk?"

"Should Melissa, be there?"

"If you wish."

"I wish, because I'm the mother of the kidnapped."

The three walk into the solarium and sit.

"What I'm about to tell you, you must forget once you hear it."

"Yes."

"Last week, Katherine Elizabeth Samuels, the former Makeda; her attorney, Eliot Livingston; Federal Corrections Officer, Robert Jones; and ten members of the Archangels motor cycle gang were killed during a botched attempted federal prison break in Wayfar, Colorado. We now know that four compatriots of Ms. Samuels escaped a very intensive shoot out with a substantial sum of money. We believe these compatriots to be Benny Radle, who now rests in a city hospital, David Ellis, Wilson Abraham, and Ernest Davis. These men, with their now-anglicized names, were soldiers in the army of Queen Makeda at the former REACH Mission. They did her dirty work.

"One or several of them were responsible for the death of your former husband, Misses Sattill. These four were closely associated with the Archangels. We believe that the money earned by the Archangels' drug deals was going to finance the escape of the queen and her four compatriots back to Ethiopia. The queen must have promised the Archangels some major level of power if they aided in her escapes. But their presence at the prison break confirmed their allegiance to the queen and her plan.

"The four men, we're convinced, are responsible for the recent deaths of Jamie Lanno, William Swarts, Joan Mussleman, and Thomas Clarkton. The perps seem to be exacting vengeance on all those who destroyed their world of crime, put them in jail, and imprisoned their beloved queen. That's why they have come back to New York. They need a lot of money. They're hot. Anyone who would illegally transport people out of this country already knows that the authorities are after the four—now three. Extraction would be extremely expensive, because the risk is so great. We know of only two or three organizations that would take that level of risk. And we're watching them. We further believe the three remaining men to be those who have your children. That's the only way they can garner enough money to buy three safe passages back to Ethiopia."

"They've asked for five million. We've stalled them as long as we can without further jeopardizing our children. They've already sent us Antonio's pinky finger to stress their resolve."

"Sir, I haven't seen anything in the news about prison break in Colorado. Why?"

"Missus Sattill, it can't be reported if there is no evidence it ever happened. Remember, we're the federal government, we can do anything we wish."

"But Tony has told me you're the federal prosecutor, not the entire federal government."

"For the public's sake, I have the title of prosecutor, but I'm really a facilitator. I have access to and can exert influence over many departments with the help of the department heads. I can function as a single point of leadership. Then when an event has passed, I know what has happened and can obliterate any paper trail. Then I return to the role of prosecutor."

"That is somewhat disconcerting."

"It is one of the ways we work. Another is with full transparency, or so the public thinks. We—er, I—saw the advantage of having Tony pursue his approach, while we stayed in the shadows. We thought he could ruffle the feathers of the four men, by agitating their queen. We need them to come into the light as a group. I was right. Tony's visit to Wayfar accelerated the process. We also had a twenty-four-seven watch on her lawyer. His trip to Colorado would be the sign that the prison break was near."

"So you have been monitoring this case and the activities of the four men for weeks, but have done nothing."

"The unfortunate murders were within the purview of the local police. We could do nothing without ruining their investigations. Our job now is to get the three remaining bad guys as rapidly as possible. When are you supposed to turn over the ransom?"

"Noon today, but we're stalling until four tomorrow."

"What say we offer a compromise? Half of the five million today. Eight p.m. at a place of their choosing. This will give us time to confirm their method of fleeing the country. Plus, we have that much bogus paper available. It'll make them happy."

"What about our children?"

"Missus Sattill, we'll acquire them in the exchange. Of that, I'm sure. If and when the perps attempt to spend the money, they'll realize that have been duped. But we hope to snatch them before that. Any questions?"

"How can you be so positive that we'll get our children in the first exchange?"

"Because they desperately need money immediately to pay for their trip abroad. They'll take any large amount immediately, with the promise of the balance within twenty-four hours."

Silence.

"Okay, this conversation never happened. Now let's find out what the others have learned?"

"Paul, Ms. Tate has the equipment to track a phone call, but her technology is not as precise as ours. We can narrow the target to a block or two. So we'll go with ours. Agent Black and I believe the NYPD simply can't do the job of finding the criminals. They're just too obvious. That's why we have called for a Tactical Strike Force in each borough to be at the ready once we receive a call. So to make this effort a success, we'll need either Mister or Missus Sattill to keep the criminals on the line for at least three minutes. Hopefully more, if possible."

"Thank you, Agent White. How can we involve the two lieutenants in the pursuit and capture?"

"When we have the meet time and place set, we'll turn over the capture to the NYPD."

"Chris, Brendan, are you guys cool with that?"

"Jenny, be sure to learn all you can about this ultra-hi-tech used by our federal friends. It'll put you light years ahead of your counterparts on the force."

Tony's telephone buzzes six times.

"Hello."

"Impotent retired Captain Sattill, where's our money?"

"Where are my children?"

"They're safe, but not for long."

"I want to speak to Cassandra."

"Ah, the black whore. How fortuitous, we have your delicious little one right here."

"Mommy, these men tried to do a bad thing to me, and they punched Bartheleme. Come quick."

"That's enough."

Melissa's face has no color. She can only imagine what the kidnappers had tried to do to her poor daughter. "Listen to me, you bastards."

"Silence. We only want to speak to your impotent husband. Sit quietly in the corner, bitch."

"Is Bartheleme injured?" Tony asks.

"Only a few scrapes. He would make a brave warrior in our country."

"Leave my children alone. Your issue is with me. I put you and your evil queen in jail. Deal with me. Come after me. Or are you too much a coward to fight man to man?"

"The best way to cause you the pain we suffered is to strike you were most vulnerable. That's why we have your children."

"Let me ask you about your queen. How is she doing in prison? Does she like it there? Can she communicate with her lawyer?"

"Silence. That is of no concern to you."

"But it is a concern to you, is it not? I'm planning a second trip to see her in Colorado. Shall I take her any messages from her three remaining soldiers?"

"Silence."

"What shall I tell her?"

"You can tell her nothing of importance."

"Okay, then let me tell you something. Here's our offer. We have in our possession two and one-half million dollars in non-sequential fifties and hundreds. We can deliver two large duffel bags to a place and at a time you declare anytime today."

"We demand five million."

"I'm not through with the offer. Along with the cash, you'll receive me as a hostage. There'll be an exchange of people. Our three children go free, and you get me. Then tomorrow, my wife will deliver the balance of two and one-half million, and you'll release me. All of this is being offered in good faith that the children remain unharmed. Do not touch Cassandra, Bartheleme, or Antonio."

"What good are you to us?"

"You talked about causing me pain. What better way that to have me before you?"

"We'll call you in one hour. Do not stray from your telephone."

છછછ

"Where are they?" Tony asks.

"In Queens driving on the BQE between One Thirty-Four Avenue and One Thirty-Sixth Avenue. They apparently stopped to talk to you. We sent our local Tactical Strike Force to that location two minutes ago. They should be calling in shortly."

"Nice work."

"Base this is TSR-Queens. We have acquired a dark green van parked by the side of the road. Now it's back on the BQE heading toward the next exit. We'll follow at a safe distance. The van is now turning into what appears to be an alley. We can't see the exit at the other end of the alley. Two black males are exiting the van. One of them is pulling a young girl by her arm. She's blindfolded. We'll sit on this location until further notice."

Tony asks himself if the bait and switch will work. He'll know in 3,600 seconds, plus or minus.

"Tony, what the hell did you just offer those guys?"

"I'm going to get our children back."

"But you're giving yourself up to a group of desperate criminals who hate you and have nothing to lose by killing you."

"It buys us time to get them. It'll work, trust me."

"Paul, can you talk some sense into his thick head?"

"With all due respect, Tony, this is a stupidly dangerous plan."

"Paul, hear me out. When they set the meet to deliver the first half of the ransom, we'll make the exchange. They will, no doubt, take me to the same place they're now holding the children, because it's their comfort zone. I will be wearing a transponder, so the NYPD can track me. It's imperative to my safety that my whereabouts be known by you at all time."

"I doubt they'll go for the offer of half a loaf. And even if they do, they'll strip search you for electronic devices. If they find one, and they will, they'll kill you immediately."

"Listen, everyone. I'll have a transponder secreted in my body, a place they won't look. Can the federal listening devices hear the ping from my nether region? If, yes, we have a plan. If not, I'll be in trouble."

"Sweetheart, you're being foolishly cavalier. I want all the members of my family safe and sound. Not just my children."

"Missus Sattill, we have a transponder that can be rectally inserted, and that we can track from a quarter of a mile. Through walls, traffic, everything. But, Mister Sattill, this transponder, because of its range, is not tiny. It's a little larger than three golf balls end to end."

"How much is a little larger?"

"About twenty percent greater diameter than a golf ball."

"Okay, Agent Black, get me one. I'm convinced these guys will take me up on my offer."

Tony goes into the bathroom to test drive the transponder. First, the lubricant on it and in him. Next, down to his knees with his face on the floor. Finally, the insertion attempt. The first time is a failure. The second attempt is a partial success, but very painful. The third attempted entry is a success with most of the device. The pain is nearly overwhelming. The pressure on Tony's colon and nearby bladder causes him to pee on the floor. He extracts the device and notices a little blood mixed with the lubricant. Now he has to crap. He sits on the bowl and relives himself. The fourth try is a success. He is dizzy from the pain and almost passes out. Tony withdraws the device and slumps onto the urine soaked rug.

"Tony, are you all right? Answer me."

"Sweetie, I'm fine. A lot of localized pain, but fine."

He wipes away the lubricant and blood, pulls up his pants, and rejoins the total team. He walks slowly and slightly bent over.

In twenty minutes, Tony's telephone buzzes six times.

"Hello."

"Impudent retired Captain Sattill we have decided to accept your offer. A life for three lives. Do you have the money with you?"

"Yes, I do."

"Good. Bring it to the building at thirteen fifty-six Jackson Boulevard in Jackson Heights, Queens. Come alone. You'll receive instructions at that point. Keep you cell phone by your side. Be there in forty minutes, or your daughter will suffer."

The second insertion ritual goes slightly easier. Tony has nothing left in his bladder.

"Tony, it's not too late to back out. We could alert the NYPD, and they could execute the capture."

"Not enough time. This is my job. Agent Black, this damned transponder better work for a quarter of a mile."

"It will, sir."

"Who will follow me?"

"Agents Black and White will be with you all the way."

"I hope their vehicle is non-descript."

"Tan Chevy four-door"

"Perfect. I'll be driving our Mercedes. Also since I'll need to keep my personal line open, I'll need a second phone to call them. Agent, enter your number on speed dial number one. When I leave the car, I will toss the phone. Let's go."

"We'll put a transponder in your car, so we can't lose you in traffic. We'll get to the address in Jackson heights before you.

"Dearest, I don't know what to say. I love you."

"Love you, too, sweetie."

Paul has had the duffle bags of money delivered to Tony's building. Tony loads them into his car's trunk. The drive to Jackson Heights is not so difficult at this time of day. Not rush hour. Tony arrives at the appointed address at the appointed time. His phone buzzes.

"Good. Now go to the corner of One Hundred Twenty-Eighth Street and Forty-Ninth Avenue in Bedford Stuyvesant, Brooklyn. You have forty-five minutes."

"But wait."

Silence.

He relays the new address to the agents. They will be there. The drive to the address in Bedford Stuyvesant takes forty-seven minutes.

"You're dangerously late. We would hate to reprimand your children because of you inability to follow instructions properly. The next and perhaps the final stop is in lower Manhattan. The corner of Broome and Arch Streets. Thirty minutes."

"That's not enough time at this hour."

"Sufficient time to save your children."

Silence.

The agents will follow. The traffic on the bridge is a like log jam. He roars around cars. Leans on his horn to warn other drivers. Blinks the car's lights to gain a slight advantage. He is there. Sweat covers his body. His heart is racing. His phone buzzes.

"On time. Congratulations. For your good work, go to one-four-four-five Second Avenue. Your children await you. By the way you have twenty-five minutes."

The two car caravan races north to an empty lot filled with the rubble of the building that once occupied the space.

Chapter 17

Tony stops the Mercedes, and watches the tan Chevy go past him and slide into a spot in front of a bodega. The agents have a clear line of sight in the rear view mirrors. Tony exits his car holding his cell phone. It buzzes four times.

"Congratulations, the delivery boy has arrived."

"Where are my children?"

"In due time."

"Now or I get back in the car and you get nothing but the fire of hell."

"Patience, impudent one."

"Let me see my children."

"Look to the back of the field to the right."

Tony spies three small bodies seated with their backs to him. They appear to be bound and tied together. He starts to approach the small huddled mass.

"Stop. Do not attempt to touch or communicate with the children."

He freezes in his pace.

"Now follow these simple instructions, and all will go well. First, get the money from the car. Second, place the bags beside you on the sidewalk. Third, remove all of your clothing including your shoes. Fourth, wait for us."

"Then my children will be freed?"

"Yes, but if you deviate from the instructions, they and you will die. We have rifles pointed at you four."

Tony examines all the windows and roofs surrounding the empty lot. There are no sniper vantage points. But he will not call their bluff and does what they want.

"All of your clothes. That includes your underwear."

Humiliation for the lives of his children is a fair trade for a father.

"Stand there with your hands above your head. Now turn around slowly."

He sees the children looking toward a doorway in the building to the right of the lot. They struggle to rise and walk toward their father. As they near him, Tony sees the fear in their eyes.

He whispers to them in great urgency, "Run, dammit, run to the car. Get in and lock the doors. Help will arrive as soon as I'm gone. Everything will be okay. Go."

When he hears three doors slam shut, he sighs in relief. His embarrassment is not a factor. He squints toward the rear of the lot as a dark green van pulls up behind him. The panel door slides open, and he is roughly attacked by two men, bound and gagged. The two duffle bags and Tony are rudely tossed into the back of the van. It heads north. The tan Chevy follows two blocks behind.

∾∾∾

In less than three minutes, a large black SUV pulls up behind the Mercedes. Melissa jumps out before it stops and runs to her babies. Two men dressed in black help the children into the SUV, while Adolfo drives off in the car. The SUV heads for Lennox Hill Hospital. ER doctors are waiting to care for the SUV's cargo.

ოჳოჳ

Melissa joins Cassandra for her examination. The female doctor is considerate and precise.

"Cassandra, did the man touch you inappropriately?"

"He touched my breasts and pulled down my panties right before Bartheleme jumped on his back and whacked him on the head. Nothing beyond that."

"You're a brave young woman."

"Not as brave as Bartheleme. He risked his life for me. How's he doing?"

"He's with another doctor in another room. When we finish your examine, you can see him. Missus Sattill, may I speak to you outside the examining room?"

"What is it?"

"Given the trauma of the attempted rape, you may want to have Cassandra see a child psychologist. I think she's okay, but emotional issues are not my area of expertise. I suggest this only as a precaution. Other than that, your daughter is in fine shape. No bruises and no breaks that are detectible. Blood work will be back in a few hours."

"Thank you, Doctor. Now I must see Bartheleme." Melissa looks into Cassandra's space. "Cassie, I'm going to check on Bartheleme. I'll be there when you're ready to see him."

"Mommy, do you realize that's the first time you called me Cassie and not Cassandra. I like it."

"I love you, Cassie."

Bartheleme is sitting up on the bed. Two practitioners are touching and looking at the patient, while they read the monitor and print outs.

"So far, your soldier is rock solid, Missus Sattill. We'll want to do an MRI to confirm no damage done by the blow to his head. That'll take another hour. Then, depending on what we find, he can go home."

"Bart, what you did for Cassie was very brave. I'm so proud of you to risk so much for your sister."

"Bart? Who's Bart? That must be me. I like it. And who's Cassie? That must be Cassandra. I'll bet she likes it."

"She does, and I'm glad you like Bart, too. Now I'm going to visit with Antonio. Your sister will be here in a short while. When she arrives, the two of you find me in the waiting room. Okay?"

"Okay."

Renaming children from the formal to the familial strengthens the bond between parent and child, as well as between the children. Nicknames like "Butch" and "Cookie" bestowed during childhood cement a bond between friends that can never be broken regardless of age or distance apart.

"Missus Sattill, we need to talk before you see your son. Despite the fact that you kept his finger on ice for two days, reattaching it will be difficult. Beyond the talents of the staff of Lennox Hill. You see the cut was not clean. It appears to have been made with multiple strikes from an ax or large knife. Certainly it was non-surgical. We have called the best neuro-surgical team in the city to attempt the reattachment. They're due here momentarily. We're prepping him for surgery. You can see him briefly."

"Antonio, how's my big boy."

"Really groggy, Mom. The doctor told me they're going to try and reattach my finger. And that they're able to do that because you kept my pinky on ice for two days. Thanks, Mom."

"Tony, you'll be fine. The best surgeons are coming here for the reattachment. See you and your ten digits when they're done."

"Love you, Mom."

"Love you, baby"

The wait starts. Cassie is the first to sit with her mother. Bart joins the women two hours later. Cassie is already asleep with her head on Melissa's lap.

☙❧

The first blow is to the back of Tony's knees. He crumbles. The second and third blows are to his right and left shoulders. These minimize his ability to fight back while producing wide spread pain. His hands are tied behind him, and a rope is threaded around and between his hands. He is then raised off the floor by means of the rope. In this contorted position his naked body hangs eight inches off the floor. He could get pain relief if he can touch the floor. Attempts are useless. He remains dangling and naked.

Still hooded, gag remains in his mouth. He is total isolated. Pain is gradually moving from his arms and shoulders down his back to his legs. Occasionally, one of the black men will face Tony and punch him in his ribs, which are beginning to slowly separate. As he drifts into unconsciousness, they burn his belly and thighs with an iron rod. He snaps awake, thus putting additional pressure on his shoulders. More pain.

Occasionally, the iron rod misses its mark and touches his genitalia. This draws great laughter from his captors. This process continues intermittently for hours. He must keep the transponder within him. If it falls out, he is lost. He must be tough. Melissa will arrive with the

NYPD version of the cavalry and save him. That's the plan.

"Oh, impudent one. The great Captain Sattill retired, will soon be the impotent one."

When they call Melissa, they hear Tony's phone ring. Confusion sets in.

"How is that possible? Dial her number again."

Same result.

"How do we reach the black whore? How do we get the rest of our money?"

"Deliver our number to her. David, you must ride to her house like Benny, and hand the doorman a letter with one of our telephone numbers. She'll call us, and we'll arrange the meeting place and time. She'll give us the money, and we'll sail away to home."

⚬⚬⚬

"Black and White to Base. The bad guys appear to be in a building guarded by a fence. The building's off the Brooklyn Queens Expressway near One Hundred Thirty-Fifth Avenue in Jackson Heights Queens. The entrance is down an alley. The dark green van is parked in the alley nose out. There's no way around the vehicle to the building. Assault is not feasible in this situation."

David Ellis loads his bike into the van and heads off to Manhattan.

"We have one bad black bird leaving the nest. It looks as if he's putting a bicycle in van. Do we follow?"

"Base to Black and White. Follow at a distance. Do not apprehend. Advise of route and destination."

"Black and White to base. Rider just delivered an envelope to Sattill's building and is heading back to the van. We'll follow."

"Paul, did your guys say an alley near One Hundred Thirty-Fifth Avenue in Jackson Heights?"

"Yes, Brendan."

"We know that place. That sounds like the entrance to the Archangels' club house. If that's accurate, we've been there."

෴

The intercom rings. Adolfo answers and goes to the lobby to retrieve the envelope.

Call 683-5839. We will tell you where to deliver the balance of our money.

He rushes to the hospital.

"Missus Sattill, you got this message."

"Thank you, Adolfo. Please take the three of us back home."

෴

Melissa is torn between the safety of her husband and the health of her child. Realizing that waiting for the results of the multi-hour operation will not help Tony, she calls the number.

"Ah, the black whore. It was an interesting trick to have all calls go through your arrogant husband's phone. Do you have our money?"

"I will have the remaining two and one-half million tomorrow before ten in the morning."

"Please give me a number where we can reach you with delivery instructions. Until then, remember we won't hesitate to cause grave bodily harm to your husband if the New York Police try anything against us. He has already begun to understand the depth of our anger toward him. Let there not be more."

"Listen, you cheap shit coward, you brutalized my children. Isn't that enough? Leave Tony alone. Call this number, five-seven-three-eight-six-seven-one. I will answer at ten tomorrow morning."

"Your husband must be made to understand how much we have suffered."

Silence. Tybor summarizes the next steps.

"I'll send a few people around tomorrow to be here when they call. My people will then notify the NYPD and will remove all this equipment. We have to be the ones that notify the NYPD. That keeps the two lieutenants and the tech officer from getting jammed up. They've been operating well below the radar."

Adolfo counters, "Sir, with all due respect, we were in this mess from the beginning, and we'll be there at the happy conclusion. You can notify the NYPD, but we'll be there and get our captain out of this jam."

Paul Tybor leaves, and Melissa and Adolfo go back to the hospital. Carmelita stays with the other two children. Melissa must wait. Wait for news. Wait for her son. Wait for her husband.

"It's kind of you to sit with me, Adolfo, but it isn't necessary."

"Missus Sattill, I feel responsible for what has happened to the children. I want to be here when Antonio comes out of surgery."

"Adolfo, you're not responsible for any of this. The people who have Tony are responsible. Not you and not Tony. Just them. Sitting here, I wish I could get my hands on the cowardly bastards who hurt three children."

"Do not fret. They'll get their just desserts."

Melissa senses an ominous tone in Adolfo's voice, but lets it go. One hour becomes two in the waiting room. It's been five hours since little Tony went into surgery, and seven hours since big Tony was traded for her children. Time is standing still. She begins to nod. Suddenly, the door to the waiting room is filled with a doctor.

"Missus Sattill, I'm Doctor Eshleman. I'm the surgeon who worked to reattach your son's finger. My team and I deem the reattachment a success. With proper bed rest and the antibiotics, he'll make a complete recovery from the operation. Then comes the rehabilitation. This will be the long, and most likely frustrating, aspect of his regaining use of the finger. Fortunately, there are several good rehab clinics in the city. I have taken the liberty of writing down the two I prefer and the names of the doctors in charge. I urge you to visit each one with your son to determine which one he likes. I also urge you to start the rehabilitation process as soon as possible. No later than a week after we're sure there's no infection. Is all this clear?"

"Yes, Doctor. I can't begin to thank you enough."

"Missus Sattill. It was your clear thinking about putting the finger in salt water and on ice that made the entire procedure easier than it could have been. We thank you. Now, your son will remain sedated this evening. You can visit him in the morning. Before noon. Goodnight, Missus Sattill."

"Goodnight, Doctor."

"Home, ma'am?" Adolfo sees the stranger and slips past him and out the door.

"Missus Sattill, may I have a word with you."

"Who are you?"

"I'm Mason Roberts of the *Ledger*. I would like to ask you a few questions about the events surrounding your child's admission to the hospital."

"I have nothing to say to you. Aren't you the reporter who met with my husband? Didn't my husband tell you to stop intruding into our personal lives? Didn't he tell you he would give you an exclusive story when all of this is over?"

"I just want to ask you a few questions on how your young son was injured. Did the kidnappers do this? What did they do to your other children?"

"Leave me alone."

"The public has a right to know what is happening to the family of a former police captain and the daughter of the former president of the city council. You're a high-profile couple that can wield a lot of influence. The people have a right to know what the movers and shakers are doing. The people have the right to know how the upper echelon of society handles kidnapping and kidnappers."

Adolfo reappears in the doorway. "Missus Sattill, is this man bothering you?"

"Yes, he is."

"Sir, would you please step aside and let Missus Sattill leave?"

"I have the right to provide the public with news."

"You don't have the right to bother Missus Sattill. We're leaving now."

Mason Roberts reaches out and places his hand on Melissa's arm. Instantly, Adolfo grabs the reporter by the head, kicks his legs from beneath him, and slams him to the floor. The reporter's head bounces off the linoleum.

Adolfo wraps his hands around Mr. Roberts's neck. "Now you have a choice. Move and have your neck broken or stay still while we leave the hospital. I will claim that you struck Missus Sattill, and that my actions were justified. Which is it?"

"I will be still on the floor."

"Good choice."

Outside the hospital, everyone can hear the siren and horn of a fire engine. It seems a car accidently caught ablaze. The car belongs to a reporter who is now screaming about suing for assault, unaware that his car is no longer functional.

"Adolfo, I don't want to know what just happened, but thank you for saving me from that rat."

"My pleasure, ma'am."

His grin is barely perceptible. The ride home is quiet. Melissa has had too much excitement for one day. She just wants to sleep in her bed with her babies safe by her side. The mother instinct is more powerful than men know.

❧❧❧

The rib punches and burning with the iron rod are less frequent during the night. The perps add a new pain-delivery system. They hit Tony's thighs and the soles of his feet with a baseball bat. Morning cannot come soon enough for Tony.

❧❧❧

Morning comes way too soon. Melissa hurries over to the hospital at six a.m. to see Antonio.

"How's my boy?"

"My left hand hurts a little. I bet it's swollen. The drug drip is working. The nurse said that I must stay here until they're sure there's no infection."

"Good morning, Antonio. How do you feel?"

"Okay, I guess, Doctor."

"Let me take a look at your finger. Everything seems to be going according to schedule. Missus Sattill, you'll able to take Antonio home most likely tomorrow. But he must stay in bed with his hand elevated for the first day he's home. Then bed rest, the meds, and some good home cooking."

"Doctor, you have never tasted my mother's cooking. It's not good."

"Tony, shush."

"'Antonio, I'll check in on you this afternoon. You seem to be a fast healer. Youth is a wonderful curative. Have a good day."

"Mom, how are Bartheleme and Cassandra?"

"Bart and Cassie are fine. They'll want to see you as soon as possible. I'll have Carmelita bring them over after breakfast. By the way, it is Bart and Cassie now. No more formal names, Tony."

"That's cool. What about me? If Dad is Tony, can I be T-Two?"

"T-Two it is then."

"Love you, Mom."

Love you, T-Two."

She heads home.

Chapter 18

It is eight-thirty. Melissa has been awake for four hours. The intercom tells her that Paul Tybor and his friends are in the lobby. Chris and Brendan are not far behind. Paul's people pack up their technical gear leaving the NYPD gear for Officer Tate. The fed techies leave. Officer Tate leaves. Paul, Chris, and Brendan remain.

"Coffee?"

Coffee all around. Melissa goes to her bedroom to dress. They must wait for the ten o'clock call.

"Chris, what is the status of the Queens tactical squad."

"They're ready, Paul. According to Borough Chief Britton, the squad comprised of two assault teams and four snipers are standing ready to control the perimeter once the bad guys come home. They estimate getting into position will take five minutes. They'll hold their positions until we arrive. Britton is leaving this on our shoulders, but when it succeeds, he wants to make the announcement to the press."

"Did you tell him what happened to the last member of the force who wanted the spot light?"

"Yes, and he said he is willing to take that minor risk."

"Brendan, are the phones and bugs in place?"

"Yes, sir."

"How about Adolfo? Has he been alerted and his duties explained in detail."

"Yes. He should be here soon."

Melissa enters the solarium.

"What is going on here?

"Mrs. Sattill. We can't give you details. But rest assured you'll be out of harm's way, and your husband will be rescued. Adolfo will drive you to wherever the perps tell you. He'll help you carry the bags of cash. So, when you see the bad guys, you must explain that the full bags are more than you can manage. That's all I can say."

The intercom announces Adolfo.

It is nine-fifteen. The big duffle bags of bogus cash sit next to the elevator door in the foyer.

They wait. Forty-five minutes, 2,700 seconds. No call.

"Where the hell are they?"

"Patience, Mrs. Sattill. Their ploy is to heighten your stress level. In the hopes you make a big mistake."

"Well, the stress part is working. But it's hardening my resolve to get these bastards and retrieve my husband. There'll be no mistakes."

The phone rings five times.

"Hello."

"Well, hello, whore. It's time for you to pay us what you owe us."

"Cut the crap, asshole. Where should I deliver the money?"

"Drive your car to the bus stop at Ninety-Eighth Street and Fifth Avenue. Be there at exactly eleven-fifteen. Come alone. We'll be watching for you and any police."

"I can't drive, and the duffle bags of money are too heavy for me to carry. So, my driver will bring me and the ransom to Ninety-Eighth and Fifth."

"I said *come alone*, bitch."

The caller's screaming could be heard by everyone in the room.

"No driver. No money. It's that simple."

Melissa is bluffing with Tony's life. Sweat drips noticeable rings in the underarms of her Yale blue T-shirt.

"All right, but once your man has delivered the bags, he must return to the car and wait for you."

"Agreed."

Click.

"Chris contact Britton. Tell him it is on."

"Adolfo, are you ready. Remember deliver and return to the car."

"Paul, Britton tells me the bad guys left their hideout thirty-five minutes ago. His men are in position awaiting our arrival."

"May I ask, why don't you send men to the delivery spot?"

"Because the bad guys are already there. They would see us and queer the exchange. Just trust us that we know what we're doing."

"Okay, Mr. Facilitator. Adolfo, let's go. Brendan, will you give us a hand loading the bags into the trunk. Paul, will you be leaving with us?"

"No. I will leave with Chris and Brendan. All will be well very soon."

The elevator never moved so slowly. Mrs. Denn and her two yipping fur balls got on at the eighth floor. Mr. Leonard with his walker got on at six. The dogs were es-

pecially hyper today, all the new smells in such a con-
fined space. Finally, the garage.

The trunk is popped and the bags are dropped in.
Brendan heads upstairs as the car exits the underground
space.

⌀⌀⌀

The drive takes eight minutes. Adolfo pulls the Mercedes into a parking spot at the corner of 96th and Madison. On Madison. The delivery is to be at eleven-fifteen
exactly. The deliverer is seven minutes early. They wait.
Tick-tock-tick-tock. At eleven-twelve Adolfo pulls out of
the parking spot and heads north to 99th street. A left and
another left point the car to the bus stop at 98th on Fifth.
The Mercedes pulls into the bus stop space. The people
waiting are upset that a car would interfere with their daily bus ride. The bus will be unable to pull to the curb.
Passengers will have to navigate the eight feet from curb
to bus. One of the men yells at Adolfo for causing such
an inconvenience. Adolfo thinks, *What pussies*. It is exactly eleven-sixteen. The bus leaves.

A white van pulls in front of the Mercedes. A boney
black man exits the passenger side door. He beckons to
Melissa. Both she and Adolfo exit the car and go to the
open trunk. Adolfo grabs the bags and walks slowly to
the white van. Melissa is beside him. After twenty steps,
they are beside the van. The door panel slides open to reveal another boney black man leaning over Tony. He is in
the fetal position. Naked, bruised, and bleeding from several areas of his ashen skin. Upon seeing Melissa and
Adolfo, he generates a slight smile. His eyes are glazed,
and he is shaking. Fever induced by the beatings.

"Put the bags down by the van and leave."

Adolfo does what he is told and gets into the car. He watches one of the men hoist the bags into the van. Then suddenly, the boney man grabs Melissa and pushes her into the vehicle. Adolfo does not move. He must wait. The van speeds away. South on Fifth, then East on 96th. Adolfo reaches for his phone.

"Chris, they have the money and Mrs. Sattill, just like you said they would. What should I do now?"

"Go back to the residence and wait for my call. Good job."

☙❧

"Did you really think we would leave you safe and secure in your sky palace? You'll be made to suffer as your impotent husband has suffered. Then we'll put both of you out of your misery."

"You fucking cowards."

The smile on the boney black man is one of earnest menace. He can wait to cause her pain. No sense in becoming agitated during the trip to the hideout. To ensure tranquility, he binds Melissa's wrists, places a gag in her mouth, and duct tapes her mouth.

She looks fearfully at Tony, who manages another small smile. He mouths the words, "I love you." His head bobs with the bumps in the roads. Melissa bounces on her butt. The trip to the hideout takes fifty minutes in lunchtime traffic.

The van is backed into the small alley. It is a tight squeeze. The only way in or out of the van is through the rear door. First one, then the second, then the third boney black man exits. Two of them grab Tony and drag him on the ground to the door of the former club house. The third man roughly pushes Melissa. Through the club house to the warehouse behind. The five are in. Three feel safe.

One has no idea what will happen. Tony hopes that whatever will happen, happens very soon.

Suddenly, the doors at either end of the warehouse are ripped from their hinges. Four flash grenades come bouncing into the high ceiling space. Tony recognizes the projectiles and struggles to cover his ears and close his eyes. As he does so, he motions to Melissa, who follows suit. Less than a second later, all four flash-bangs explode. Blinding white light and deafening explosions are followed by large billows of smoke. Immediately, each doorway is breached by four men wearing assault gear and masks.

The unarmed boney black men can do nothing but obey the commands to lie face down on the floor with their hands outstretched. Capitulation is complete.

"Ma'am, are you all right?"

Melissa can barely hear Chris. He gingerly peels away the duct tape and extracts the gag.

"Stunned, but fine, thanks."

She looks at Tony, who is being treated by an EMT as Brendan watches nervously. Two officers wrap Tony in a blanket as they await the gurney. Melissa slowly walks over to one of the hand-cuffed bad guys and kicks him in the face. Blood gushes from his mouth and nose. He cries out in agony. Then she approaches another and stomps on his groin. He passes out from the pain.

The third perp sees what has happened and cowers and whimpers. He receives a kick to the ribs. She hears what she thinks is the splintering of bone as the perp doubles over gasping for breath, and then he screams. Melissa's self-defense martial arts training is finally useful. As she moves to Tony, she muses that no one tried to stop her assaults on the three men. The police stood and watched in awe.

"Doctor, is he okay?"

"Ma'am, he has multiple contusions over his body, open wounds on his arms, legs, and genital area, and he is suffering from damage to the shoulder muscles. Plus he is dehydrated and most likely has not eaten for a few days so his resistance to infection is low. In a nut shell, he is very banged up. But he is strong and will make it. I'll know the exact extent of his injuries when I get him back to the hospital. How do you feel?"

"My eyesight and hearing are approaching normal. I'll be fine."

"I want to examine you back at the hospital, also."

The three perps are loaded into a police van, while Tony and Melissa are placed in the EMS Wagon. Different modes of transportation. Different destinations. Tony and Melissa to Lennox Hill hospital. The three perps to the Tombs, pre-arraignment holding cells beneath One PP.

⋘⋙

Melissa's examination takes twenty minutes. She moves to the waiting room. Chris and Brendan are already there.

"What did the doctor say, Mrs. Sattill? He has yet to examine Tony."

"My eyesight and hearing are back to normal. Now tell me, Chris, what the hell just happened?"

"Paul figured that the perps would take the money and return to their hideout. We knew where that was so we had it locked down before they returned. We never thought they would take the money and you. Their actions were a surprise to all of us. But we got them, and you and Tony are okay."

A small lie to cover the truth of a fuck up.

"I am, for sure. I want to wait for the doctor to finish his examination of Tony. I'll call Adolfo to come here and keep me company. If you two want to go home, please feel free to leave."

"We took the liberty of calling Adolfo. He should be here any minute."

"Brendan, it seems that you two have thought of everything."

"We had a great teacher."

Through the doorway walks Adolfo. He sits. The four wait for Tony's doctor.

☙❧

The three black men are walked through the booking process. Mug shots. Finger prints. Strip searches. Clothes and shoes thoroughly examined. They are escorted naked to the showers and told to scrub real hard. After towel drying, they dress and are escorted to three cells apart from the general population also awaiting arraignment. These men are special. And they are given special names—Number One, Number Two, and Number Three.

"I need a doctor. My ribs were broken by the she-bitch black whore."

"You'll all be examined when the doc arrives tomorrow at seven. Now shut up and put your clothes on."

"Seven? I could bleed to death by then."

"Tell your lawyer during your one phone call. I'm sure he'll expedite the process—or not."

"I have no lawyer."

"Then, as you understood when arrested, one will be appointed for you prior to arraignment. You can call legal aid. The number's next to the telephone. Your lawyer may come tonight or sometime tomorrow. The court is very busy and almost bogged down with all the perps and skels coming through the system. So suck it up, little buddy."

By the time the boney black men arrive at the Tombs, all the officers know who they are and what they have done to Tony, one of the true blue, and his family. These bad guys will get the average, run-of-the-mill police bureaucratic slow dance through the process.

Three phone calls. Three legal aid lawyers arrive around six that night. The six men huddle in one interview room. No one cares to listen, because everyone knows the three black men will get the max after a brief trial.

"Officer, my client needs immediate medical attention. His ribs were broken during the arrest—police brutality, and he is bleeding internally."

"Doc Jones is in the infirmary. I'll escort your client there now, if you have completed your consultation."

"Yes, that will do."

"Come on, scum, the doctor is in."

"What about my client? He has a broken nose," another legal aid lawyer chimes in.

"I'll call for another guard, and we'll take them both."

The arrival of the second guard takes twenty minutes. No sense in hurrying.

The guards and perps walk slowly to the infirmary.

"Doc, we got a couple crybabies here. This one says he was beaten up by the police when he was arrested. I heard a woman kicked his ass. This other one claims the police hit him in the face with the butt of a rifle. Same woman kicked him, too. I didn't realize that Queens had women on its tactical squad."

While the doctor examines perp Number One, a guard handcuffs perp Number Two to a chair that is bolted to the floor.

"Number One, lie on the examining table. When I press, tell me if it hurts and how much on a scale of one-to-ten with ten being the most severe. Do you understand?"

"Yes."

The process is gradual and not precise. The most severe pain is around the last two ribs on the right side.

"I don't think there's real damage, but I want to take an X-ray to be sure. Get up and move to the machine."

The guard helps the perp to the machine.

"Just as I suspected. The bottom two ribs are fractured. Clean breaks. Nominal bleeding. I'll tape you and then you can go back to your cell. That woman must have had a helluva kick."

The doctor examines Number Two. A broken nose at the least. More than likely several sinus bones are also cracked. Tape is all that can be administered. He thinks, *Jesus I don't want that woman angry at me.*

ഇ๛ഇ๛

"Mrs. Sattill, we have completed the examination of your husband. He has suffered an extensive beating and all the damage that entails. Hematomas, muscle tissue damage, and bone shifting. He also has burns on his penis and scrotum. Plus his shoulder muscles have been stretched extensively. He will need a great deal of rest and rehabilitative therapy, and perhaps surgery to address the shoulders. We have him under pain medication and fluid to rehydrate his system. If you want, you may see him now. He may not be responsive, and you can't stay long. Follow me."

The hospital cleaned him up. The ashen flesh and the large dark bruises create a macabre image of Melissa's once-robust husband. The sight makes her gasp.

"Tony, can you hear me?"

A slight nod.

"We got all the bad guys. Chris tells me they're being processed and will be arraigned tomorrow. I'll be there for the family." She leans over to whisper in his ear. "It was a rush. A painful rush, but pure adrenalin nonetheless. I kicked the motherfuckers. I felt great. Now get some sleep. Adolfo will be outside tomorrow if you need anything. I'm going home a going to bed. I truly love you. You're my knight in shining armor."

When Melissa arrives home, she excuses Carmelita and prepares for the onslaught of questions from her children.

"Is Dad okay? Are you okay? When can we see him? Did you get the kidnappers?"

Each question is answered in order and with as much detail as reasonable for teens. After forty-five minutes, Melissa retires to the bed she shares with her beloved. Now empty. Sleep is instantaneous, deep, and long. Carmelita's arrival awakens her.

"Where are the children?"

"In their rooms."

Melissa calls the school and explains the extended absence of her children. The headmaster is sympathetic. Melissa promises that they will be back in the classroom the following Monday.

∽∾∽∾

On the steps of One Police Plaza, Queens Borough Chief Alston Britton holds a press conference for all the media outlets. "I'm pleased to announce the capture of three hardened criminals. Yesterday afternoon, a joint task force led by the Queens Hostage Rescue Squad, raided the hideout of Benny Radle, David Ellis, and Wilson Abraham and subdued them after a fierce fire fight. Fortunately, no one was killed or severely injured. The three men had been previously incarcerated in connection with the REACH Mission criminal enterprise here in Manhattan fifteen years ago. The fact that they were paroled from prison before their sentences were fully served is a question for the judiciary. These three men had kidnapped and held for ransom a retired police captain and his wife. It was only through diligent and skillful police work of these men behind me that we were able to locate the whereabouts of the hostages and secure their freedom. These men deserve all the credit, and they'll receive accommodations accordingly. I will now take questions."

Melissa turns off the television and says to no one, "That lying bastard. First, he throws the legal system under the bus. Then he takes full credit for everyone else's work. He's obviously running for a major office. Not if I have anything to say about it."

She can't be late for the arraignment.

The courtroom is crowded. Many more reporters than usual. Judge Schriver has to use his gavel several times to quell the noise.

"Docket number ending in nine-four-one-two. The people versus Benny Radle, David Ellis, and Wilson Abraham. The charges include kidnapping, illegal restraint and containment, attempted murder, conspiracy to commit murder, resisting arrest, possession of firearms by convicted felons, and battery on a police officer."

"If it please the court, for the defense, James Snyder, Ann Rimpo, and Jules Marteen. We're all from the public defender's office.

"Mr. Snyder, how does your client plead?"

"Not guilty on all counts."

"And your client, Ms. Rimpo?"

"Not guilty on all counts."

"And your client, Mr. Marteen?

"Not guilty on all counts."

"Miss Harwill, what's the position of the People on bail?"

"The crimes and those to be itemized in future indictments are heinous. The ransom money they sought was to be used by the defendants to flee the country. We request these criminals be held without bail in the Riker's Island facility until trial."

"I agree."

Judge Schriver bangs his gavel once again. The men are lead away. The three defense counsels approach the assistant district attorney.

"Miss Harwill, we'd like a meeting with you to discuss reducing the charges and thus the punishment."

"A meeting will be fine with me. Then I'll tell you about how your clients kidnapped three children. They attempted the rape of a twelve-year-old girl. They beat a fourteen-year-old boy, and they chopped off the finger of a fifteen-year-old boy. Your clients are the poster men for evil and depravity, and they're going away forever. Now, do you still want to meet?"

Harwill could tell, by the oh-my-god expressions on the faces of the three lawyers, that their clients had conveniently omitted their other criminal acts.

"We'll get back to you."

They walk away with slumped shoulders, defeated before they start.

"Miss Harwill, my name is Melissa Sattill."

"Yes, I know who you are."

"I want to ask that you keep my children out of this as much as possible. The public scrutiny would simply be too much, given what they have been through."

"Mrs. Sattill, rest assured I have no intention of introducing at trial the evil that was set upon your children by these three men. I was simply using the threat of introducing the vile acts to gain control of the defense. You and your husband will have to testify, if it even comes to a trial. I'm hoping to clean up this mess and send them away for life without the time and expense of a trial."

"Thank you. Now if you'll excuse me, I want to see Tony."

"Before you go, I have a question. I would like to see if you can confirm the rumors that someone kicked the crap out of the three criminals. I have been told that the kicker was a woman. Do you know anything about that?"

"Nothing at all. I was recovering from the flash-bang grenades when the three were subdued. I could not see or hear anything. Now, I really must go."

Melissa's facial expression gives her away.

Both women have sly grins on their faces—Harwill, because she just confirmed the rumor, Melissa, because her reputation as a kick-ass wife and mother is growing.

⁂

In the belly of the Tombs, the three boney black men are shackled and loaded on the bus that will take them to the Riker's Island facility. The bus is crowded and stinks of sweat and disinfectant. The ride takes forty-five minutes. Processing begins anew.

⁂

"Tony, how do you feel?"

"Better than last night, but I still hurt all over. The tubes and the meds are testimony to my healing process. The doctor says I'll have to stay here for a two more days. Then a few weeks of intensive rehab and a follow-up examination of my shoulders. I might need surgery. How about you?"

"I survived the bang-flash grenades. I'm at one-hundred percent."

"How are the kids holding up?"

"They're strong and resilient. I think I would like Cassie to see a psychologist just to be sure there are no permanent scars. Maybe the boys, too."

"Camp will be a good escape for them. Can't say they can't go after all they've been through. When can I see them?"

"This afternoon. I have let them stay home from school for a few more days to get back to normal. Whatever that is."

"I guess our reunion trip is out of the question. Mostly, because I don't want to leave the children. Letting them leave us for camp is a different story."

"I agree."

Melissa notices Tony's eyes are beginning to close. Fatigue is winning the battle. "Honey, I better go. You look like you could use some sleep. Besides the doctor told me to keep visits brief, but they can be frequent. I'll be back later today with the children."

She leans over to give him a kiss.

"I'll have the band here when you return."

By the time she gets to the door and turns around, Tony is asleep.

৩৩৩

When she enters the lobby of her building, she notices a familiar but dislikeable man sitting on one of the leather couches.

"Well, Mason Roberts. How unpleasant to see you."

"Mrs. Sattill, I have a few questions. The hospital would not let me even in the building to see your husband. They had guards escort me out of the building. I guess absolute privacy is what money and influence can buy."

"Stop!" Melissa's loud response echoes through the lobby. "I have no information or comment for you at this time. I believe my husband promised you an interview after the ordeal was over. Only he can determine when it is over. So, no comment is all you'll get from me."

As if from nowhere, Adolfo appears. He walks silently to Melissa's side.

"Mr. Roberts, you remember Adolfo, don't you? I believe you two met at the hospital. Thank you, Adolfo. Mr. Roberts was just leaving."

Mason Roberts leaves as Melissa and Adolfo enter the elevator.

"Children, your father would like to see you. He's well enough for a brief visit this afternoon. So, shower and get into presentable clean clothes. Not the home alone rags you have on now. Carmelita will get lunch ready. We leave at one. Adolfo, please join us. I know Tony would like to see you."

લ્જાન

The troop enters the hospital. The children are carrying "Get Well," "Come Home," and "We Miss You" balloons.

The joy and love that emanates from Tony's room for the next half hour makes the floor and station nurses smile. A hundred questions are asked and answered. Kisses abound. Cassie cries until she hugs her daddy. The thirty minutes is over all too quickly. Back to the car and home.

"Your father and I agreed if you still want to go to camp, you should."

"Why would we not want to go?"

"Bart, we were just concerned that you may not have wanted to be away from your parents after what you went through."

"Mom, please. We can't wait for camp to get away."

"Okay, then it's unanimous. Camp it is. The reunion trip for your father and me is another story. Your father will not be strong enough to travel by Memorial Day. So I have canceled the trip. Your grandparents were disappointed but insisted that they come over to visit."

Melissa realizes she has yet to inform Tony of the new names for the children. Tomorrow.

Chapter 19

The coverall-clad orderly moves quietly through the NYU General Hospital hall and into each room to remove the trash from the baskets. Once the trash is collected, he will squeegee the floor of the room and hall. His is a menial job. No one pays much attention to him or his activities. The young police officer at the doorway to Ernest Davis's room is reading a book while he guards the prisoner, who is shackled to his bed. The orderly passes by the officer.

Once in the room, the orderly removes a syringe from his side pocket. He walks deliberately to the bedside. Ernest Davis stirs slightly. The night visitor inserts the needle into Davis's neck and injects nothing but air. It will take a few moments for the air bubble to reach the brain and work the intended magic of death. The orderly withdraws the needle. There is no blood at the insertion spot. The syringe is placed back in his pocket, and the orderly leaves the room.

The night visitor takes the elevator down two floors and slides into the trash collection closet. He removes his coveralls, beard, and wig and tosses them down the trash shoot. He then casually walks back to the elevator. Once outside, he enters a big Mercedes and drives off.

ℰᏬℰᏬ

New York Ledger Friday, May 2, 2014
Three Commit Suicide at Riker's Island
The three men recently arrested on charges of kid-napping were found hanged in their cells at the Riker's Island prison early this morning. Benny Radle, David El-lis, and Wilson Abraham apparently hanged themselves using their bed linen. Prison officials investigating the three separate incidents said that suicide is an unfortu-nate outcome of remorse.

ℰᏬℰᏬ

The huge arrangement of flowers requires two order-lies to carry into Tony's room. It takes up almost one en-tire wall. The card nestled amongst the stems reads, *It's over*. There is no signature, but Tony recognizes the reach and the power of "The Face."

About the Author

John Andes was born and raised in Central Pennsylvania and received a degree in philosophy from Brown University. His business career, centered on advertising and marketing, started in New York and moved to various cities in the US. He has written the entire spectrum of B2B and B2C marketing communications. Andes has two adult sons, is retired, and lives on the Florida Gulf Coast. He coaches little league football, mentors small business owners and entrepreneurs, and teaches creative writing. Andes has authored *Farmer in the Tal, Suffer the Children, Icarus, Matryoshka, Jacob's Ladder, Loose Ends, Control is Jack, Revenge, Adventures in House Sitting, Skull Stacker, Street Cleaners, Hidden Agenda,* and *Question Everything…Then Dig Deeper*. His web page is www.crimenovelsonline.com

www.ingramcontent.com/pod-product-compliance
Lightning Source LLC
Chambersburg PA
CBHW070447120726
47910CB00003B/958